The Giver

AMISH COUNTRY BRIDES
Christmas

Jennifer Spredemann

© 2020

Published in Indiana by *Blessed Publishing*.

www.jenniferspredemann.com

All Scripture quotations are taken from the *King James Version* of the *Holy Bible*.

Cover design by *iCreate Designs* ©

ISBN: 978-1-940492-56-8
10 9 8 7 6 5 4 3 2 1

Get a FREE short story as my thank you gift to you when you sign up for my newsletter here: www.jenniferspredemann.com

BOOKS by JENNIFER SPREDEMANN

Learning to Love – Saul's Story (Sequel to Chloe's Revelation)

AMISH BY ACCIDENT TRILOGY
Amish by Accident
Englisch on Purpose (Prequel to Amish by Accident)
*Christmas in Paradise (*Sequel to *Amish by Accident)* (co-authored with Brandi Gabriel)

AMISH SECRETS SERIES
An Unforgivable Secret - Amish Secrets 1
A Secret Encounter - Amish Secrets 2
A Secret of the Heart - Amish Secrets 3
An Undeniable Secret - Amish Secrets 4
A Secret Sacrifice - Amish Secrets 5 (co-authored with Brandi Gabriel)
A Secret of the Soul - Amish Secrets 6
A Secret Christmas – Amish Secrets 2.5 (co-authored with Brandi Gabriel)

AMISH BIBLE ROMANCES
An Amish Reward (Isaac)
An Amish Deception (Jacob)
An Amish Honor (Joseph)
An Amish Blessing (Ruth)
An Amish Betrayal (David)

AMISH COUNTRY BRIDES
The Trespasser (Amish Country Brides)
The Heartbreaker (Amish Country Brides)

The Charmer (Amish Country Brides)
The Drifter (Amish Country Brides)
The Giver (Amish Country Brides Christmas)

NOVELETTES
Cindy's Story – An Amish Fairly Tale Novelette 1
Rosabelle's Story – An Amish Fairly Tale Novelette
2

OTHER
Love Impossible
Unlikely Santa
Unlikely Sweethearts

COMING 2021 (Lord Willing)
The Teacher (Amish Country Brides) book 6
Title TBD (Amish Bible Romance)
Title TBD (Amish Bible Romance)
Title TBD (Christmas book)

BOOKS by J.E.B. SPREDEMANN

AMISH GIRLS SERIES
Joanna's Struggle
Danika's Journey
Chloe's Revelation
Susanna's Surprise
Annie's Decision
Abigail's Triumph
Brooke's Quest
Leah's Legacy
A Christmas of Mercy – Amish Girls Holiday

Unofficial Glossary
of Pennsylvania Dutch Words

Ach – Oh

Bann – Shunning

Boppli/Bopplin – Baby/Babies

Bruder/Brieder – Brother/Brothers

Daed/Dat – Dad

Dawdi – Grandfather

Denki – Thanks

Der Herr – The Lord

Dummkopp – Dummy

Englischer – A non-Amish person

Fraa – Wife

G'may – Members of an Amish fellowship

Gott – God

Gut – Good

Jah – Yes

Kapp – Amish head covering

Kinner – Children

Kumm – Come

Maed/Maedel – Girls/Girl

Mamm – Mom

Ordnung – Rules of the Amish community

Rumspringa – Running around period for Amish youth

Schweschder(n) – Sister(s)

Wunderbaar – Wonderful

Author's Note

The Amish/Mennonite people and their communities differ one from another. There are, in fact, no two Amish communities exactly alike. It is this premise on which this book is written. I have taken cautious steps to assure the authenticity of Amish practices and customs. Old Order Amish and New Order Amish may be portrayed in this work of fiction and may differ from some communities. Although the book may be set in a certain locality, the practices featured in the book may not necessarily reflect that particular district's beliefs or culture. This book is purely fictional and built around a fictional community, even though you may see similarities to real-life people, practices, and occurrences.

We, as *Englischers*, can learn a lot from the Plain People and their simple way of life. Their hard work, close-knit family life, and concern for others are to be applauded. As the Lord wills, may this special culture continue to be respected and remain so for many centuries to come, and may the light of God's salvation reach their hearts.

ONE

"Oh, no! Not again!" Bailey Beachy Miller waved her hand in front of her face, attempting to dispel the smoke. She coughed several times, turning away from the plume that should have been apple pies for her family and her almost-fiancé, Mark.

She wanted to cry. After four years of using her stepmother Nora's woodstove, she thought mistakes like this were in her past. Apparently not. Oh, how she missed the commercial stove *Aenti* Jenny used in her bakery. Or the gas appliances in *Mamm* and Silas's home.

Not that she minded living in her *vatter*'s stricter Amish district. There were just certain nuances she'd had to adjust to. Like having to cook on an old-fashioned woodstove.

She surveyed the blackened apple pies again and huffed. Mark would have to go without a treat this week, unless... She snapped her fingers and smiled. That was what she'd do. She'd stop by and visit *Mamm* and *Aenti* Jenny today, and pick up a treat for Mark and dessert for the family, while she was there. Problem solved.

It had been quite a while since she'd visited her other family. She'd gotten so busy with life and helping out with *Dat* and Nora's *kinner*, that time had slipped by. They would be happy to see her, as she would be to see them, especially since the winter months could soon leave them homebound. Not that they *couldn't* get out if they really wanted to, they just tended to stay closer to home more.

"Whoa! What happened in here, Bay?" Her *vatter*, Josiah, coughed as he brought a load of firewood inside.

"I burnt the pies." She sighed, shoulders sagging.

"More like burning the house down." He frowned. "Distracted again?"

"Not really. I set the timer. I guess I set it for too

long. Or the heat wasn't right."

"Doesn't Nora have a recipe in there somewhere?" He pointed to the recipe box her stepmother kept on the counter. "She should have the baking times written down."

"I know. I just have a hard time keeping the temperature regulated on this stove."

"You adjust it by how much heat you allow into the oven compartment by using that lever. I thought I showed you." He stacked the wood in the rugged box designed for that purpose. Keeping plenty of firewood on hand inside the house prevented extra trips outside, curtailing the amount of cold entering their home.

"You did. I still can't get it right." She frowned. "I miss Mom's stove."

"Ah, I see. Looking for the easy way," he teased.

"It *was* easy compared to this. Sometimes I wish this district had the same allowances."

"I know. But wishing does no good. You know that."

"I don't know how you adjusted back after being an *Englischer* all those years."

"Well, I grew up this way. It was second nature to me." He stared down at the pies and grimaced. "You know, when you and Mark are married…"

"I know!" She covered her face with her hands. "He's going to think I'm a horrible *fraa*."

He squeezed her shoulder. "No, he won't. Stop being overdramatic."

"Well." She shrugged. "I guess he'll just have to learn to like burnt food."

"Should I warn him?" *Dat* teased.

"Don't you dare!" She threw a pot holder at him. "Besides, contrary to current circumstances, I *can* cook. And bake. And I'm pretty good at it."

"Should we open up some windows in here so Nora and the *kinner* can breathe when they get home?"

Bailey rolled her eyes. "Very funny, *Dat*."

"Humor aside, it would probably be best if they didn't come home to a biohazard zone."

"Humor aside, huh?"

Bailey paused before entering Millers' Country Store and Bakery. *Ach*, she had such *gut* memories here. She remembered barely being able to see over the counter when *Mamm* and Silas first opened the store. She'd been about six at the time, so she'd spent a *gut* deal of her life here. And she had an extra layer of softness to prove it.

The moment she opened the door, sweet aromas assaulted her senses. Vanilla, cinnamon, and fresh-baked bread wafted through the air of the small establishment.

"Oh, good! Bailey!" Her aunt Jenny swooped around the service counter and briefly embraced her. "I need you! Can you come work?" Was that desperation in her aunt's voice?

"Right *now*?"

"*Jah*." She moved back behind the counter and returned to the task at hand.

"Oh, uh, well I didn't—"

"What was your *mamm* thinking, going and having a *boppli* just before Thanksgiving and Christmas? Our busiest time. I've had about a dozen people come in just this week, asking for her potpies. I don't know how to make them! I think your *mamm* must use some special ingredient in

5

hers because mine never turn out the same. Just ask your *onkel* Paul."

Bailey couldn't hold in a giggle. "I don't think *Mamm* can control when the *bopplin* come."

"She has more control than you realize." She held up an angled icing spatula and eyed Bailey with curiosity. "You'll be married before too long. Hasn't your *mamm* talked about...well, you know...*that*?"

Bailey's cheeks suddenly warmed. "*Ach*, you know *Mamm*. She was an *Englischer*. I've probably heard more about *that* than any *maed* in this community." She laughed.

"*Nee*, I don't think I'll ever forget your *mamm* was *Englisch*." She shook her head and chuckled. "Or *my Englisch* days. Your *onkel Paul* still wishes I'd wear...*ach*, never mind." She swatted the air in front of her.

Bailey laughed. "But you were never really *Englisch*."

"Right. Just pretending for a brief time."

"Did it feel strange?"

"It did. Part of me liked it. Or, liked the

attention it brought from your *onkel* Paul, I should say." She lifted a mischievous smile. "But the other part of me hated it. It just didn't feel like me. You know what I mean?"

"I think so. When I went with *Dat* to New Jersey to help him move from his condo, it all felt very weird. It was like I was in a movie, being around all those fancy people. Especially when he took me to his office. It was in one of those expensive shiny buildings way up in the air. I got to ride in an elevator many times when we were there. That was kind of fun."

"*Jah*, maybe." *Aenti* Jenny continued icing the gigantic pan of cinnamon rolls. "But I would never want to live in the city."

"Neither would I." Bailey went to the sink in back and washed her hands. "What would you like me to do? I can stay for about an hour."

"Will you make up some of your *mamm's* potpies for me? I can bake them, if you can't stay that long."

"Okay, I can do that. I'm supposed to meet Mark at the library later on."

"Really? You two are pretty serious, *ain't so*?"

"*Jah*, we are, but..."

Aenti Jenny stopped mid-spread and stared at Bailey. "But what?"

Bailey shrugged. "How do you know that you're marrying the person you're supposed to? I mean, it's for life. It's not something you want to get wrong."

"I know all about that."

She opened the cupboard and found the mixing bowl. "*What*? I thought you and *Onkel* Paul got along great."

"Oh, no. I wasn't talking about your *onkel*. My first beau." She shook her head. "I'm just glad I met Paul when I did. And at that time, I knew that *Gott* had brought me to him. Although I wasn't sure how He would work out the details." A fond smile flashed across her face. "But He did." She studied Bailey carefully. "Are you having second thoughts about this Mark fellow?"

"I don't know. It just feels different, I guess."

"Different than what?"

"From my first beau."

"Ah, I see. Timothy Stoltzfoos, right?"

"*Jah.*" She frowned. Her heart still felt like someone held it in their hands and squeezed it like one of those squishy stress balls. Fortunately, like the stress ball, her heart would eventually return to its normal state.

"He's single now, you know."

"He is?" She gave her head a firm shake. "It doesn't matter. Timothy left me. Besides, Mark and I are practically engaged."

Aenti Jenny's gaze probed her. "But you still have feelings for Timothy, *ain't not*?"

"*Ach*, how could I not? I thought we would marry. We *would* have been married by now. I was devastated when I found out about him and MaryAnn Kinsinger. But like I said, it doesn't matter. I don't think I'd ever take him back. Not that he'd even *want* me back."

"You never know." *Aenti* Jenny shrugged. "I don't know if I should tell you this or not, but..." Her voice trailed off.

Bailey planted a fist on her hip. "Oh, no. You are *not* going to tease me and then not tell."

"It's just that, on church Sundays, I always notice Timothy's gaze searching the women's side. It always starts with your *mamm* and me, then drifts toward where the single *maed* sit." She pulled her bottom lip between her teeth. "I think he's looking for you. And when he discovers you're not present—again—he looks away, like he's discouraged or disappointed."

"*Ach, Aenti* Jenny. Don't tell me that." When a tear surfaced, Bailey couldn't help being frustrated with herself. She was past Timothy, wasn't she?

"You insisted."

"I know, but..."

Aenti Jenny nudged her with her hip. "I think he still loves you, Bailey."

"No, he doesn't." She shook her head as she mixed in the flour with the other ingredients for her pie crust. "Love doesn't do what he did."

"*Jah*, but everyone makes mistakes."

"It wasn't a mistake! He *deliberately* chose MaryAnn over me." *Ach*, now she was all worked up. She turned away so *Aenti* Jenny wouldn't see her tears. Why did Timothy's rejection still sting so much after all these years? "Can we not talk about him anymore, please?"

Bailey's hands shook as she rolled out the dough for the pie crusts. Why had she gone and dredged up old feelings for Timothy again? She was past that, or at least she thought she had been.

Aenti Jenny had grown quiet, likely praying for her.

When a customer entered the store, Bailey's head snapped up. *Good, it's not Timothy.* Because seeing him at this moment in time wouldn't be *gut.*

TWO

An hour later, Bailey said goodbye to her ever-so-grateful aunt.

Since Mark had heard she'd be near town, he'd wanted her to meet him at the library. It worked out perfectly with her. She had a couple of books she'd been wanting to check out. Besides that, she adored this library. The creamy-yellow brick building appeared quite ancient, and the library's name looked to be spelled in medieval-type font. The only reason she'd known that was because she'd once read a book about a medieval princess, that had its own special alphabet in the back. The letter style appeared similar to this. But the thing that she loved most about this library was the inside. The large comfy chairs and couch beckoned her to slip a book from one of the shelves, slide into a comfortable position, and shift her attention to another world.

But she wouldn't have time to do that today. No, Mark had something planned for the two of them, he'd said. Excitement simmered inside at the thought of Mark wanting to do something special. It seemed he'd been so busy with work lately that they barely spent time together. An evening alone with Mark would be a nice treat.

She'd arrived ten minutes early, so she decided to take a stroll up the block. She loved the old Methodist church building on the corner. It had been made with the same brick as the library, but was even more exquisite. Beautiful crosscut windows, a spire that seemed to reach to the heavens, and what she imagined to be a gigantic bell. *Ach*, how she loved when the bell sounded throughout the streets of the town! It was often a familiar hymn, but around this time of year, Christmas carols rang loud and clear from the stately dome.

She waited patiently, knowing that at the

beginning of the next hour, music would reverberate throughout the small town. She wished she had a way to tell time. If her driver's vehicle clock was correct, she'd arrived early, but the next hour was quickly approaching.

And then it happened. The strains of "Hark the Herald Angels Sing" wafted through the crisp air. She stared up at the cross on the steeple, chills prickling all over her body. There was something majestic about the entire experience, like God Himself was present in the music, or at least listening. Just her and God, reveling in the delightful carol bringing glory to His name.

A vehicle whizzed by, breaking through her meditation.

Ach, it was past five o'clock. Surely Mark was already at the library.

Bailey hastily crossed the street and rushed through the double doors, immediately enveloped in warmth. She walked through each section of the library, but Mark was nowhere to be found. *So he hasn't arrived yet?* Glancing at the clock on the wall, she realized it was already five minutes after. It was rare for Mark to be late.

"Bailey?"

She spun around at the familiar voice. *Timothy*. Suddenly her cheeks heated and she felt out of sorts.

"I thought that was you!" He dared to move close and, before she realized it, he'd enveloped her in an embrace. Right there in front of the librarian's checkout station! *Ach*. Definitely *not* proper Amish behavior, especially in a public place. Had he noticed her rigid stance as he pulled her unwitting self close? What had he been thinking?

"I haven't seen you in forever," he gushed.

She was too *ferhoodled* to even speak. *Ach*, he was even more handsome now than he'd been when they'd courted. But she shouldn't be thinking about how *gut* looking Timothy was. She shouldn't be thinking about his mesmerizing blue eyes that she used to get lost in. She shouldn't be thinking about how his masculine scent seemed to linger on her woolen coat.

"What are you doing here?" His perfectly formed lips asked. She shouldn't be thinking about those either. *Ach.*

"Books," she managed to squeak out.

"Oh, okay." He stared at her bookless arms, seemingly puzzled.

"I-I need to get them." What she meant was she needed to get away from *him*. Fast.

"Do you mind if I come with you?"

No. Yes! Bailey squeezed her eyes shut. Could he be more maddening?

"Is there a Bailey Miller here?" A female voice from behind the checkout counter called out, rescuing her from imminent embarrassment.

Good. A distraction. She *needed* a distraction.

She turned to the woman, once she found her voice. "I'm Bailey Miller."

"You have a phone call." The woman held out a cordless phone to her.

"Oh, I do? Thank you." Bailey took the phone. "Hello?" She spoke into the receiver.

"Hey, Bailey. It's Mark. I'm still at work and I can't get away. Can we take a raincheck on our date?"

"*Ach. Jah*, for sure. If you're still working."

"Great. *Denki*." The phone abruptly clicked off.

She stared at the silent phone a few seconds before handing it back to the library attendant.

"Is there a problem?" Timothy was at her side. Again.

"*Nee*. I just—"

"Mister Stoltzfoos?" An *Englisch* man ambled around the front desk from the stairs behind it that led to the library's lower level. He carried a large cardboard box in his arms. "I've located those boxes you asked about."

"Thank you, Mr. Williams. I appreciate it." Timothy shook the man's hand as soon as he set the box down on the floor beside them.

"There are several more of these in the basement. Feel free to help yourself to as many as you need."

"Thank you." Timothy smiled.

Bailey had always loved his smile. But she shouldn't be thinking about his smile.

Timothy turned to Bailey, disappointment evident in his mien. "I'm sorry, Bailey, but I've gotta go now."

"Okay."

"Can we...uh, on second thought, do you have a minute or two? I could use some input."

"I...uh..." But she no longer had an excuse because Mark wasn't coming. On the other hand, she did need to find a driver to take her back home. Still, she uttered, "All right."

She had no idea why she agreed to follow him down the stairs to the library's lower level. But she was curious about what he was doing. Curious what the *Englisch* man had been talking about. Curious about what was inside the gigantic cardboard box he'd given Timothy.

"See these boxes here?" He pulled out a shoebox from a larger box like what the *Englisch* man had been carrying. "They were all donated by people in the community."

Her eyes scanned the room. They appeared to be the only patrons on the library's quiet lower level. "What are you doing with them?"

"Well. We're supposed to wrap each one in Christmas wrapping paper, then we'll..." He left off speaking and walked to a table by the wall. He handed her a half sheet of paper from a stack.

She glanced down at the paper.

"We choose an age, then we buy simple gifts to fill up the boxes with." He pointed to one of the sections. "See? Here's the suggestion for, say, a four-year-old boy."

She read the list. "A small toy such as a ball, stuffed animal, a toy car, or musical instrument. Clothing, such as a shirt and pants, undergarments, scarf, hat, gloves, socks and shoes. Craft items may include a coloring or activity book and crayons or markers, stickers, finger paint, play dough, notebooks, craft kits. Personal items like a toothbrush, hair brush or comb, washcloth, bar soap, blanket."

Bailey smiled at Timothy. "It sounds interesting. What is it for? Who do these go to?"

"Poor children in other countries. They also encourage people to include a personal note and maybe a picture."

Her eyes widened. "You would include a photo?"

"Not of myself, of course, but maybe I could

get a postcard from our area so they could see what the other side of the world looks like."

"And you plan to fill up *all* these boxes?"

"Not just me. I'll probably fill a couple of them. There's a sign-up sheet up at the front desk. I also put up a few of the fliers the organization sent. I hope we'll get a lot of volunteers to fill them."

Excitement sparked from somewhere within. "I'd like to fill one," she blurted out.

"*Wunderbaar*! My first volunteer." His smile stretched across his face, and their gazes connected.

Bailey quickly looked away. No, she *would not* acknowledge the pounding in her heart. Nor would she acknowledge the jolt of electricity. No, she'd do well to remember how Timothy had left her with a broken heart.

"So, where are you going after this?" He set the paper back on the table.

"Home. I still need to call a driver."

"Oh. Well, my driver's here already. He could take you home."

"Uh, *nee, denki*. I will hire someone else."

"Don't be ridiculous, Bailey. There's no need

to call someone else, when there's already a driver here."

Bailey frowned. "You think I'm ridiculous?"

"No. That's not what I meant." He grimaced.

"I'll find my own ride." She abruptly whirled around and marched back toward the stairs.

Timothy's firm hand on her shoulder halted her in her step. "Bailey, wait."

She spun to face him, exasperated. "What?" She ground out the word.

"I just...I don't want to say goodbye to you yet." His previous smile had completely vanished. "And I don't want you to leave upset."

"You know, Timothy, that's funny." But she exhibited no signs of humor. "Because you had *absolutely* no problem with saying goodbye or upsetting me four years ago."

His shoulders sagged. "Bailey, can't you understand? I had given up hope. I thought you had left and were becoming *Englisch*. I *only* started dating MaryAnn because I had to get my mind off you. I was upset. I thought *you* had given up on us."

Ach, he was such a *dummkopp*! "I never became *Englisch*, Timothy. I went to New Jersey with my *vatter* to help him move and to see my *grosseldre* in Pennsylvania. After we returned, I moved to my *vatter*'s Amish district because I couldn't stand the thought of seeing you and MaryAnn together." She couldn't help the sob that escaped her lips. Why did it still have to hurt so much? "You promised me, Timothy! You promised me you'd wait."

"*Ach*, I'm sorry, Bailey." He dared to reach a hand to her shoulder again.

She quickly shrugged it off. "Sorry? You *said* you loved me, Timothy. And then not even *a month* later, you were with MaryAnn."

"But it was because I thought you were dating an *Englischer*. How was I supposed to know it was only your *vatter* you were spending time with?"

"I went to the singing to try and talk to you. Do you remember? You totally blew me off. And then you left with MaryAnn." She didn't know if her tears formed because of frustration or of the heartache of reliving those moments over and over again in her mind. Perhaps it was a mixture of the two. "You could have come to me and asked, instead of just assuming I'd jump into the car of the first *Englischer* that came along."

"*Nee*, I couldn't. I couldn't bear to. And then when you left to go to New Jersey... You told me you would never become *Englisch*—"

"And I didn't. I didn't even drive my *vatter's* fancy car, even though I *could* have." Her frown deepened. "I kept *my* promise!"

"Bailey..." His voice softened, then he sighed. "I'm sorry. I was wrong."

"*Jah*, you were."

"You'll never know the regret I feel. The feelings I had for MaryAnn never came close to the love I had for you."

Hadn't she been thinking the same thing about Mark? She shoved the thought away.

"You don't even know what love is, Timothy. Love doesn't just leave the minute something goes wrong. Love doesn't just assume the worst of someone. Love gives them the benefit of the doubt."

"I realize that now, Bailey." He hung his head. "Can we just start over? Please?"

"*Nee*. I'm promised to someone else now." It wasn't exactly true. They'd talked of marriage, but Mark hadn't officially asked yet. "But even if I wasn't—"

"Who?"

"I don't think you know him. He's from my *vatter's* district."

"I know a lot of people."

"Mark Petersheim. Why do you want to know?"

He shrugged. "I'm not sure."

"Have you met him?"

"*Nee*."

"Well, he's a nice guy. The kind of person who isn't going to assume things and will keep his word." Although he hadn't shown up for their date tonight. But he'd called.

"That was low, Bailey."

Her gaze narrowed. "*Jah*, it was." But they both knew her comment didn't refer to what *she'd* said.

"Bailey, I said I was sorry." He opened his

hands to expose his palms.

"Fine. You're sorry." She shrugged.

"I want another chance."

"*Jah*, well. We all have wanted things we couldn't have." Her accusing stare was aimed at him. *Ach*, how she hated her tears. Timothy didn't deserve to see how he'd hurt her—how much he'd meant to her. Not when he could so easily disregard their relationship.

Bailey rushed toward the stairs without looking back. She determined she'd hide away until Timothy left. Because she couldn't stand to think of what would happen if she gave him another chance. She wouldn't be able to endure Timothy ripping her heart out again.

THREE

Timothy could kick himself. Why on earth had he attempted to get Bailey back after seeing her for the first time in years? He couldn't be any more of a *dummkopp*. *Nee*, if he'd had his wits about him, he would have begun by building a friendship with her. Starting slow. Instead, he'd rushed headlong into asking for another chance—and straight off a cliff. Or was it into a wall?

Ugh. Had he learned nothing?

If only he'd left off with the shoebox project. She'd seemed just as excited about it as he was. Which made him fall in love with her even more. They had similar interests. They both desired to help others. They were the perfect match.

If only he could get Bailey to see that.

Gott, please help me to get Bailey back. Uh, I mean, if it's Your will. And please help the children's shoebox project to be a success.

That was what he would do. He would throw himself into the charity. If he did that, at least he wouldn't be thinking about the mess he'd made with Bailey. But all was not lost. He had realized something about her in the brief time they'd spoken. Judging by her body language and her actions, she was still just as much in love with him as he was with her. And that fact alone gave him the boost of confidence that he'd needed to hold on to hope.

He'd pondered their meeting the entire ride back home from the library. One thing in particular stuck in his mind. Mark Petersheim. Who was this guy who'd won his Bailey's heart? Was he even worthy of her?

It's not like you are. He released a disparaging sigh, but chose to bury the self-deprecating thought. *No one* was good enough for Bailey. He knew that. But did this Mark guy realize it?

Maybe Timothy would find out.

As she washed the dinner dishes, Bailey did her best to push thoughts of Timothy to the back of her mind. If only Mark had been at the library when he was supposed to be. Then none of that meeting with Timothy would have happened.

But then she wouldn't have heard about the poor children in other countries who would get a shoebox full of blessings this year. It was a *gut* thing that Timothy was doing.

He'd always had a heart of gold, it seemed, especially where *kinner* were concerned. On church Sundays in times past, she'd noticed that he'd always round up the *kinner* and play games with them. He took special care with the ones who were shy or not as popular, invoking a smile, then getting them to join him and the others. That was one of the things that had drawn her to him in the first place. Surely, he'd make a *gut vatter* someday.

Ach, there she went again, thinking of Timothy. She shouldn't be dwelling on the type of *vatter* he'd make. It was none of her business or concern now. But she *was* kind of glad he wasn't courting MaryAnn, or worse, married to her. She hadn't been right for him.

Bailey sighed. She *really* needed to refocus.

What was Mark doing right now? Was he still working? That was one thing he was good at. He prided himself on making a *gut* income. Surely, if they married, she'd never lack for anything. Not that money was all that important to *her*. *Nee*, she'd rather have love and happiness than riches.

"Bailey, someone's here to see you." Her *vatter* popped his head around the wall that separated the dining area from the living room. "It's Mark."

Ach. The perfect distraction from her wayward thoughts.

"I'll be right there." She wiped her wet hands on the dish towel hanging on a nearby hook. Too bad she didn't have a hand mirror in the kitchen so she could take a peek at her reflection. Oh well.

Mark's face lit up the moment she walked into the room. He still wore dirty clothing, so she guessed he'd just gotten off work.

"Hey, you." He stood on the rug next to the door.

"Would you like to have a seat?"

"Nah, I'm dirty." He glanced at *Dat* and Nora, who spoke quietly, likely in their own little world. Nora held Andy, Bailey's youngest half-brother, in her arms.

"We could talk at the kitchen table," Bailey suggested. "Are you hungry?"

"Let's just step outside?" He angled his head toward the door.

"*Jah*. Let me put on my coat and scarf." She reached toward the hall tree and quickly donned her outerwear.

Her three-year-old half-brother, Noah, walked up to Mark and reached his hands toward him. "Pick me up?" His bright eyes waited in anticipation.

"You're a little old to be held, *ain't not*?" He said in *Dietsch*. "Besides, I'm all dirty."

Noah stared wide-eyed at Bailey and she smiled at her little brother. "I'll hold you later, okay?" She rubbed the little one's back to reassure him. He walked over to their *vatter*, who scooped him up

Jennifer Spredemann

into his arms and blew on his belly, eliciting a giggle from the boy.

Mark walked out the door and Bailey followed. Immediately, a burst of cold air slammed into her face. She adjusted her scarf up further on her neck and covered her nose.

"Sorry I stopped by so late, but I wanted to see you and make sure you had gotten home all right." He pointed to his buggy. It had to be one of the fanciest in their district. "Let's sit in there. I kept the heater on, so it should be nice and toasty. We could go for a short ride, if you'd like."

"Okay. That sounds *gut.*" The moment she stepped up into the buggy, she gave thanks for the enclosure and the fact that their district allowed for heaters inside their buggies.

Mark untied the horse, then joined her in the buggy. "It's nice in here, isn't it?"

"*Jah.* It feels *gut.*"

"I tell you, work was crazy. We had three semi-trucks full of logs come in that all needed to be processed today." He shook his head. "I barely had time to swallow my sandwich at lunch. Which reminds me, did you make my pie?"

She grimaced. "Yes and no."

He set the horse in motion, backing up, then turning onto the deserted country lane. "What does that mean?"

"I *attempted* to make your pie but it kind of ended in disaster."

"Oh, no. Your stepmother's stove again?"

She nodded. "But I can't blame the stove. It's me. I can't figure out how to keep the temperature regulated."

"I hope you figure it out soon. I'm not all that fond of charcoal." He chuckled.

She scrunched up her nose. "That makes two of us."

"Well, when we get our place, I'll make sure you have a stove that you can cook on." He reached over and squeezed her hand. "How was your day? Other than your pie baking mishap?"

"It was...interesting." She stared out into the darkness. Their immediate surroundings were illuminated by just the yellow flashing lights of the carriage.

"How so?"

She loosened her scarf, sliding it from around her neck. "Well, first, I stopped by at *Mamm's* store, where my aunt Jenny enlisted me to make potpies."

"And those turned out?"

"Well, I just assembled them. *Aenti* Jenny was going to bake them, because I was supposed to meet up with you and I didn't want to be late. But if I *would* have baked them there, they would have turned out. It's just Nora's stove that pains me so."

"What did you go to the store for? That's a little out of the way, isn't it?"

She nodded. "It is. But I wanted to get a pie for you since mine didn't turn out."

His grin widened. "So you *do* have a pie for me."

"See, that's the thing. I *did* have a pie for you, but I forgot it in the driver's car when she dropped me off at the library."

He snapped his fingers. "I can't win for losing, can I?"

Bailey laughed. "You and me both."

"And then you went to the library?"

"I did." She released a wistful sigh. "I got to hear the church bells ring."

His lips twisted. "Aren't they a little out of tune?"

"No more than Petey Schwartz." She giggled.

"Bailey!" Mark laughed. "I can't believe you said that."

"But you're not denying it." She thrust her pointing finger in his direction.

"Have you ever known me to be a liar?"

She shook her head. "Oh, there was something I wanted to tell you about."

"What's that?"

"Have you ever heard of the shoebox ministry?"

His brow lowered. "Shoebox ministry?"

"*Jah*, they fill up shoeboxes with gifts like toys and clothes and necessities, then they send them off to other countries where poor *kinner* live."

He frowned. "Ah, I don't know if I would trust that sort of thing."

"Why not?"

"How do you know that it's actually going where they say it is?"

"Well, from what I read about it, sometimes the children send a letter back to you."

"Hmm..."

"Would you like to fill up a shoebox to send away?"

"Ah, I don't think so. That's not my thing."

"Oh." Bailey frowned as disappointment sank in. "I planned to fill one up."

He shrugged. "You can do that."

Bailey wanted to ask about the future. What if she wanted to support the ministry after they were married? Would Mark discourage it, or worse, would he forbid it altogether? The thought was disheartening.

"I was thinking it would be a *gut* project for *kinner*." Their future *kinner*. Bailey eyed Mark carefully to gauge his reaction. "It could show them how blessed they are. And they would feel *gut* about helping out another *kind* in need."

Mark nodded slowly. "A project for the school?"

"Or like maybe in the future? With our own, *Gott* willing."

Mark grimaced, shaking his head. "I don't think I'd want my hard-earned money going to that sort of thing."

"But—"

"Don't worry, I'm sure they have a lot of other people donating. They don't need our money too."

And just like that, Bailey's joy plummeted. Mark had shut her down. She couldn't help but compare Timothy's enthusiasm for the project with Mark's reaction. Hadn't Timothy said he'd planned on filling up several boxes?

The remainder of their evening went all right, but Bailey's mood turned melancholy. She allowed Mark to do most of the talking and nodded or said the minimal amount of words he needed to hear so he knew she was paying attention. But her heart hadn't been in it.

When they pulled up to her house, Mark turned to her. "I wanted to let you know that I'll be working long hours over the next couple of days."

"Even on Saturday? You don't usually work at the mill on Saturday."

"*Nee*, I don't, but it might become more of a regular thing if business keeps up the way it is. Just think about it, Bailey. The more I work, the more money we'll have. And I aim to start building us a place soon, so we'll certainly need the extra cash. I figure the way things are going, you and me could marry next year. What do you say?"

Ach, now her head was spinning. "Uh, *jah*, sure," she mumbled the somewhat intelligible response. But her words held no excitement.

"Great, then." He squeezed her close, oblivious to her mood. "I guess I'll see you Sunday, then."

"*Jah*." She opened the buggy door, then hurried to the house, not even looking back to see Mark drive off as she usually did.

Because, right now, all she could think about was being married to someone who never had time for their family and was only interested in building bigger barns for himself. And the thought was downright depressing.

FOUR

"Oh, Bay. I forgot to tell you yesterday. Your *mamm* called and left a message for you at the phone shanty," her *vatter* informed her as she walked into the kitchen to help Nora prepare breakfast.

Bailey yawned and stretched her arms wide. She'd slept fitfully last night, likely due to her warring emotions. "What did she say?"

"She was hoping you would fill in for her at the bakery while she's tending to their new little one."

"*Ach*, I saw him yesterday when *Mamm* dropped by the store. He's such a little doll baby! I could just hold him in my arms and stare at him all day."

"Well, I don't think she needs you there to stare at him."

"Funny, *Dat*."

"She said the sooner you could come help out your aunt Jenny, the better."

"I know. Poor *Aenti* Jenny! She was beside herself yesterday. They're backed up on orders and she doesn't know how to make *Mamm's* potpies."

"Well, I called back and told her you could come on one condition. That you bring back some of those delicious baked goods your aunt makes and a couple of your *mamm's* potpies."

"You didn't!"

Dat laughed. "No, I didn't. But I *do* hope you'll take pity on your old *dat* and bring some home anyway."

"We'll see. There's a good chance there won't be any extra, if they're as busy as they seem."

"I'll be praying to the contrary."

"I don't know." She teased. "I might get spoiled working over there with those fancy ovens. I may not want to come back."

"Oh, I think there might be other things that lure you back here." *Dat* winked.

What he meant was Mark. But to tell the truth, she was a little disappointed with Mark right now. And Mark was totally oblivious to her tumultuous feelings, which meant he didn't really *get* her. She wasn't about to tell him about her encounter with Timothy. Besides, there was nothing to tell.

Mark *did* know that she once had a beau whom she'd been close to, but he'd never met Timothy or anything. Nor had he seemed all that interested or concerned about her proclamation at the time.

"I can help tomorrow, then maybe next week too, if you and Nora don't mind."

"It'll be difficult." *Dat* sighed. "But I think we may survive."

"Very funny." She shook her head. "I'm sure you and Nora will enjoy some extra moments alone."

Dat quirked a half-smile. "And what makes you think that?"

"Your silly expression, for one thing." She waggled a finger at him.

"So, do you think you'll be staying at your mother's the entire week?"

"I don't know. It'll probably depend on how busy things are."

"If you do, I'm sure your *mamm* will appreciate the extra help with all those little ones."

"*Jah*, I know she will."

Bailey pulled the reins, bringing Peanut Butter to a halt behind Millers' Country Store and Bakery. She hopped down to unhitch the animal.

"*Gut* boy." She patted the horse, then spun around when she heard footsteps approaching.

"Let me take him to the barn," *Onkel* Paul offered. "I think he'll be happier with the other horses."

"*Jah. Denki.*" She watched as her uncle crooned to the horse.

"How's everything over in your neck of the woods?"

"*Gut.* The crops are in and *Dat*'s been hauling in a lot of firewood from the back acreage."

"What about you?" Her uncle's brow quirked up, and his eyes sparkled with something akin to mischief.

"What about me?" she bantered, knowing the intention of his question.

"Rumor has it, you have a beau. A pretty serious one."

She frowned.

"Wait. What was *that* look about?"

She shrugged.

"Trouble in paradise?"

"I don't know. Just some things we have to work out, I suppose."

"Things?"

"Mark works a lot. I just think that when we get married maybe he won't have much time for his family."

"Ah. I see. That's important." He nodded. "There's a *gut* chance that could change once you're hitched. I can't stay away from your *aenti* Jenny, and now that we have the *kinner*, there isn't much that can keep me gone."

"And see, that's the thing. You were like that *before* you and *Aenti* Jenny were married. Mark isn't."

"Well, there's something to say for a

hardworking man. Sure beats a lazy one that won't provide for his own."

"*Jah*. I guess you have a point. But shouldn't there be a balance?"

"True. Have you talked to *Der Herr* about it, Bailey? Maybe this Mark fellow isn't the right one for you."

"I don't know." She sighed.

"You never know. *Gott* might just have a whole different path planned for your life. Either way, you shouldn't be in a hurry. *Der Herr's* timing is perfect." He hopped into her buggy. "Well, I better get old Peanut Butter put up. I'm sure he's deserving of some oats."

"*Jah*, he is." She smiled and waved to her uncle as he drove up the driveway toward the house. He'd always been a favorite person in her life.

Only now, she was beginning to realize how much she missed being here in her mom's Amish community. She adored her *vatter* and his family, and had enjoyed getting to know him these past few years, but maybe now...

She shook her head. No, she wasn't going to let

her mind travel down that road.

What is Your will for me, Gott?

Bailey's mood took a turn for the better the moment she stepped into the store. "*Mamm*! What are you doing here?"

When her mother turned around, a tiny bundle was nestled in her arms. "Bailey." Her *mamm* smiled and they exchanged a quick side hug. "I was hoping you'd come."

"Aren't you supposed to be resting?" Bailey had trouble taking her eyes off the precious sleeping infant in her mother's arms.

"Silas gave me permission to take a short walk to the store so long as I don't start working. Besides, I knew Jenny would want to see the little one."

"And just in time too, Kayla," *Aenti* Jenny said. "I just put everything in the oven." She reached her arms out. "Let me see that sweet *boppli*."

Bailey gasped. "*Ach*, I was wanting to hold my baby *bruder*! I hardly get to see him."

45

"Look at you," Bailey's *mamm* said in a baby voice. "The ladies are already fighting over you." She handed the baby off to Jenny.

"Just wait until Martha and Emily come." Jenny gently swayed her hips, the baby snuggled in her arms. "They'll never let you see him."

"Not if I can help it." Bailey stared at the wee one, yearning to hold him.

"Don't you worry, *dochder*. You'll get your turn." Her mother eyed her. "Are you spending the night?"

"Not tonight. I have quite a bit to do at home before church on Sunday. But I was thinking I could stay here during the next week, if it's okay with you and Silas."

"You know I would love to have you here. And your *brieder* and *schweschdern* would be over the moon."

"And Silas?"

"You know your step*dat* still considers you as his own. You're the daughter of his heart. You'll always be his girl."

"I know, I just feel like..." She sighed. "Did I

hurt his feelings when I decided to go live with *Dat*?"

"I don't think so. He realized that you needed time to get to know your *vatter*. I think he was able to put himself in your shoes."

"I know he was upset with *Dat*, though."

"Yeah, we both were." Her mother grimaced. "But we're over it. We hold no grudges against your *vatter*."

"I know."

The baby's tiny cry drew their attention back to *Aenti* Jenny, who seemed to be lost in baby world.

"I think Caleb's getting hungry. He's trying to eat my finger." Aenti Jenny laughed.

"*Jah*, it's about that time." Her mother took the baby from her aunt's arms. "Sorry, Bailey. It looks like you'll have to get your baby time in later."

"Ah, really?" She frowned.

"Don't worry. He'll be all yours at lunchtime. Come up to the house and I'll fix you a nice lunch." She heaped several blankets over the *boppli* to keep the cold out.

"*Denki, Mamm.*" She watched longingly as her mother stepped out the door with the little bundle of happiness cuddled in her arms.

"Just wait until you have your own."

Bailey turned at her aunt's voice, a smile tickling her lips. "I can't wait."

A thought occurred to her just then. *Did Mark like children?* She recalled his reaction to little Noah, and worry gripped her. She wanted someone who adored *kinner* like she did.

"Well, we best get to work. We have quite a bit to do."

Bailey discarded her unhappy thoughts. There was work to be done. She moved next to her aunt at the back sink and washed her hands. "Do you have a list?"

"I do. It's on the fridge. If you'd like to start on the bread first, so it can rise, then work on the pies, that would be *wunderbaar*." *Aenti* Jenny pulled out a hefty stainless-steel bowl. "I'm going to start the cinnamon rolls."

Bailey examined the list. "*Ach*, we're making pretzels now, too?"

"*Jah*. Lots of folks have requested them. But we're only making them twice a month."

"I bet Mark would love one."

"*Jah*. Your *onkel* Paul does, for sure and certain. But he needs more than one, so you better take Mark two."

"I'm afraid I'll be taking home all my earnings in baked goods." Bailey laughed.

"Well, at least we get it at cost."

"Right." Bailey looked up as an *Englischer* walked in. "Do you want me to run the register?"

"If you could, that would be *wunderbaar*." Her aunt smiled. "I'm going to get so much more done now that you're here. That is, as long as we chat *and* work at the same time."

FIVE

*A*s soon as lunchtime rolled around, Bailey made her way to the main house—the place where she and *Mamm* took refuge all those years ago.

The moment she stepped inside the home, memories assaulted her. From the first time she looked up to see her mother and Silas kissing in the kitchen, to the tender moments she and Timothy had shared in each other's presence at the dining room table or snuggled on the sofa in the living room. She mentally relived the times her entire family played games together, enjoying snacks, and laughing throughout the evening, simply enjoying each other's company.

Ach, how she missed it all! Only now, she

realized just how much.

Jah, she loved her *vatter* and his family. But this...*this* was home. This *felt* like home.

"Bay wee!" Three-year-old Emma hopped down from the bench at the table and ran to her.

Bailey bent down and scooped her youngest half-sister into her arms. "Did you miss me?"

She always spoke in Pennsylvania German when speaking to the youngest ones, who wouldn't formally learn English until they attended school. But she knew they understood quite a bit since the adults often spoke English.

"*Jah*. I always miss you."

"That's because she doesn't visit enough," Silas's voice carried from the kitchen.

Onkel Paul walked into the living room just as Bailey and Emma entered the dining area. "Jenny stayed back?" he asked.

"*Jah*. She said someone should stay in case a customer showed up. I told her I'd try not to be too long."

"In that case, I'll take my lunch at the store." Her uncle winked, donned his coat, and stepped out the door.

"I can't blame him. I'd want to be near *mei fraa* too." Silas chuckled. "Have a seat, Bailey. Your *mamm* made some delicious chicken noodle soup."

Her mother smiled. "How do you know it's delicious?"

The side of his mouth lifted. "Paul and I *may* have snuck a taste when you weren't watching."

Mamm gasped. "You did not!"

Silas's gaze flitted to Bailey and he seemed to be holding in a laugh. "I guess you'll never know for sure and certain."

Bailey slid onto the bench next to little Emma and across from her five-year-old half-brother, Aaron. The older six, Judah, Shiloh, Sierra, Daniel, Lydia, and Lucas were all in school. This would be Judah's final year before he began helping Silas full time in the shop and on the farm.

As Bailey bowed her head for Silas's silent prayer, she gave thanks to *Der Herr* for both of her wonderful families. Just as Silas promised, *Mamm's* soup was delicious. Especially with a slice of fresh buttered bread to go with it.

"So, what's been going on in the Beachy household lately?" Silas asked before indulging in a bite of *Mamm's* aromatic bread.

"Well, *Dat*'s been cutting a bunch of firewood. He's been doing a lot of stuff around the house. Since he was on his own for so long, he was used to washing dishes, doing his own laundry, cleaning, and all that. Nora fusses when he does too much around the house, saying he's going to work her out of a job." Bailey laughed. "But *Dat* can't sit still, so if he isn't helping in the house, he's finding things to do in the shop. But he won't let us go in there right now. I'm thinking he's making something special for the *kinner* for Christmas."

"He should come hunting with Paul and me sometime."

"I'm not sure *Dat* likes hunting all that much."

Silas chuckled. "What your *dat* doesn't like is what comes *after* the hunting. It takes someone with a strong stomach to prepare the animal afterwards."

"Right. *Dat*'s not a butcher."

"Well, tell him he's welcome to come along

when we go turkey hunting next week. Have him call if he's interested."

"When will you go? I think he might be more apt to go turkey hunting than for deer."

"I need to talk to Paul and check our orders. I'm thinking mid-week, though. Tell him to invite Mike too. Everyone will need a turkey for the upcoming holidays."

"Okay, I'll do that." Bailey smiled.

"It'll be nice for the four of you to spend time together," *Mamm* mused aloud.

"*Jah*, I know." Silas said. "Maybe the ladies will come along too and you can have a sisters day."

Mamm nodded. "That would be fun."

"I can just imagine the house full of *kinner*." Bailey laughed. "Not that it isn't already when everyone is home."

"*Jah*, it can get pretty crazy. I'll admit it's a blessing that most of them can be in school during the day, but I can't say I'm not looking forward to the day when Shiloh will be home full time."

"I bet she's a big help."

"She is. But she still has two years of school yet.

And Sierra is right behind her with three years, so I'll have two helpers soon." *Mamm* smiled. "Too bad *you* aren't around more. It's nice having you here. And *not* just because you're filling in at the store." *Mamm* reached for her hand and squeezed it. "I miss you, Bailey."

When tears clouded *Mamm's* eyes, Bailey stood up and moved to give her a hug. "Would you like me to come back?"

"*Ach*, Bailey. I don't want to steal you away from your *vatter*."

"I don't think he'll mind as long as I visit fairly often. Besides, I think you need my help a lot more than *Dat* and Nora do. I could either be at the store or help with the little ones. Or we could rotate."

"Oh, Bailey, I'd love that!"

"I mean..." She glanced at Silas. "If you and Silas want that."

"You know you're always welcome in this home, *dochder*," Silas said.

"Well, okay then. Let me talk to *Dat* and Nora. I'm thinking maybe after Thanksgiving. But until then, I could still come and work at the store during the week."

"You're not planning on going back and forth in the buggy every day?"

"*Nee.* I thought maybe I could drive over on Monday and stay with you during the week, then drive back on Friday."

"That sounds like a *gut* plan." Silas nodded, then stood from the table. "Well, I don't know about you two ladies, but I should probably get back to the shop. Those orders aren't going to fill themselves."

Bailey turned as Silas kissed *Mamm* on the cheek and thanked her for lunch, then he stepped outside.

"I need to get some *boppli* time in before I go back to the store." Bailey grinned. "Is little Caleb awake yet?"

"Either way, you may hold him. He's a deep sleeper." *Mamm* took Emma's and Aaron's bowls from the table and started cleaning up.

Bailey began to help clear the table, but her mother protested. "Go ahead. Go get him. Your *aenti* Jenny will be needing you soon."

"*Ach*, okay." She spun around and headed into the living room.

"Don't weave, Bay wee!" Emma called after her.

She turned back and swooped down to enclose her baby sister in a hug. "I'm going to come back next week and I'll get to spend lots of time with you then, okay?"

"Okay." Her bottom lip jutted out.

"I'll tell you what. If there's room and *Mamm* says it's okay, I might even sleep in your room. How would you like that?"

"I *wuv* that!" Her eyes twinkled with joy.

"Okay, but right now I need to go hold the *boppli*."

"*Bopp wee*." The little girl grinned from ear to ear.

Bailey pecked her on the cheek and disappeared as soon as *Mamm* distracted Emma. She silently entered *Mamm* and Silas's room and made a beeline for the cradle. The light on the baby monitor told her that everything she said to the *boppli* would be heard on the receiver in the kitchen. She attempted to stay quiet as she lifted baby Caleb out of the cradle and into her arms, then left the bedroom.

Since the *boppli* was still asleep, she figured she'd wait until he awakened to change his diaper. *Mamm* had been right. Caleb did sleep through everything.

Bailey examined his tiny fingers, which still had extra peeling skin on them. *Ach*, she couldn't wait to have her own! "You're such a sweet *boppli*," she spoke softly and leaned down to kiss his hand.

The little one was so light, holding him in her arms was effortless. She studied his miniature features, adoring each curve of his perfect little face, trying to decide whether he favored *Mamm* or Silas. If she recalled correctly, he resembled Daniel when he was a *boppli*.

Mamm joined her on the couch about ten minutes later. "I just put the other two down for a nap. Aaron was all tuckered out. He worked 'really hard' helping *Dat* and *Onkel* Paul this morning, he said." *Mamm* smiled.

"Are *bopplin* always such a joy?" Bailey couldn't seem to tear her gaze away from the little one.

"I think so. They are to me, at least." *Mamm* gently stroked the *boppli's* fine hair. "It all depends on how you look at it and what your attitude is. I guess it's that way with just about everything. You can see things or people in your life as a blessing or as a curse. I choose to see them as a blessing."

"I try to."

"But?"

Bailey sighed. "I ran into Timothy at the library the other day."

"And?"

She didn't know why, but her eyes seemed to automatically fill with moisture. She shook her head, not trusting her voice.

Mamm frowned. "You still love him, don't you?"

"I've *tried* to forget about him. For a long time. And then I thought maybe Mark could be the one. But when I saw Timothy again..." She brushed away a tear. "I don't know. I don't think

I ever stopped loving him, *Mamm*."

"What are you going to do about it?"

"I don't know. Mark's been talking about getting married next year. I've tried to love Mark and to think of him the same way that I did...that I *do*...Timothy. But it just doesn't work."

"Love should never be forced, Bailey."

She glanced down at the *boppli* as he began to stir. Probably a result of hearing his *mamm's* voice. "But love isn't all about feelings, is it?"

"Right. It's much more than feelings. But that doesn't mean you *won't* feel. Do you understand?"

"I think so. And that's just the thing. It's not just feelings. I love Timothy. Everything about him." She shook her head. "Well, almost. I don't think I can ever trust him again after what he did."

"Do you think Jesus trusted the disciples after they betrayed and abandoned Him?"

Bailey shrugged.

"He did. He trusted them enough to spread the Gospel, His Gospel. The Bible says the disciples turned the world upside down." *Mamm* squeezed her hand. "We all have times when we fail. I'm sure Timothy regrets the choices he made back then, *ain't not*?"

"He said he was sorry." But still...

"And does he desire a relationship with you?"

"*Jah*." Her heartbeat quickened. She couldn't actually be contemplating another relationship with Timothy. She couldn't. She wouldn't.

"Then it looks like the ball's in your court."

"I can't just breakup with Mark, though. I mean, we've been dating for nearly a year and he's constantly bringing up marriage and—"

"You need to pray about it. Ask God to open the doors He wants you to walk through and ask Him to close the ones He doesn't want you to enter."

"But how will I know?"

Mamm stared at her. "You'll know, *dochder*."

Bailey shook her head and sighed. *Jah*, she would pray. But trusting Timothy with her heart again was something she didn't think she'd ever be able to do.

Gott, please show me the way.

SIX

As Bailey rode home alongside Mark in his carriage Sunday evening, she did her best to shove the conversation with *Mamm*, *and* the one with *Aenti* Jenny, *and* the one with *Onkel* Paul, out of her mind. Not an easy feat. Especially after tossing and turning the past two nights, trying to forget about Timothy.

She *had* been praying though. She hadn't prayed about the door thing, like *Mamm* suggested, but she did pray for clarity and direction.

Ach, she didn't know what to do. But she knew that she couldn't just break up with Mark. She didn't really have a valid reason, did she? It's not like she planned to go running back to Timothy anyhow.

She liked Mark. He was safe. He wasn't going to lead her on, pretend he was going to marry her, then skip off with the first *maedel* that caught his eye. That was not who he was.

Of course, she hadn't thought that was who Timothy was, either. And then he showed his true colors.

Why did love have to be so complicated?

"You're awfully quiet tonight." Mark reached over and squeezed her hand.

"*Jah*, I have a lot on my mind."

"We can talk about it."

She shrugged. "You know I'm spending the week at my *mamm's*, right?"

"*Jah*, you mentioned it earlier. It's fine with me. You know how busy I've been at work lately. I probably won't even miss you."

I probably won't even miss you? Wow. Ach, did Mark even love her? Was Timothy missing her right now?

The truth was, she probably wouldn't be missing Mark, either. What did that say about their relationship? Were they just together because it was comfortable? Or because it was expected of them? Or was she just having second thoughts because she crossed paths with Timothy again?

Bailey sighed.

"I probably won't come inside tonight." Mark maneuvered the rig into her driveway. "I've got to get up early tomorrow, so I should probably go to sleep."

"*Jah*. Okay."

"I'm guessing you'll probably want to get to bed early too, since you're going to your *mamm's* tomorrow."

"Right."

"Do you want me to walk you to your door?" He glanced her way.

"*Nee*, that's not necessary."

He brought the horse to a stop close to the front door. "Okay, then. Sleep tight, Bailey." He leaned over and pecked her on the cheek. "See you. I don't know when, though, with both of us so busy. Maybe Saturday night or next Sunday?"

"*Jah*. Okay. Goodbye, Mark." She scurried from the warm enclosure of Mark's buggy to the front door of the house, then stepped inside.

For the life of her, she couldn't figure out why, but she felt like melting into a heap and having a *gut* cry. Wasn't she supposed to be happy after spending time with the man she'd be marrying? But all she could think about was his words.

I probably won't even miss you.

Today was the day.

Timothy had been asking around, putting his feelers out in the community, to see if anyone had heard of or knew this Mark Petersheim guy. Of course, he *could* have just asked Bailey's family, but he didn't want to do that. He didn't want it to get back to her. She was already upset enough with him.

He wished he had more information about the guy. He could kick himself for not asking Bailey where he worked. That would make locating this Mark fellow much easier.

He'd asked in his community and had gotten nothing so far. Maybe he should go to Bailey's community and ask. Surely *someone* there would know.

Ach. He smacked his forehead. *Of course!* Why hadn't he thought of that before? His *daed* owned a copy of the Amish directory for the area. Surely Mark's family would be listed, along with their address. *Daed's* copy was a fairly recent one, so everything should be up to date, unless their family had recently moved.

Timothy went to *Daed's* desk in the living room.

"*Ach*, I didn't know you were in the house," *Mamm* said from the kitchen breezeway.

"*Jah*. I wanted to look something up in the directory."

"Very well, then. I've got lunch on the stove, so I better get back to it before it boils over."

"I probably won't be here for lunch, but I'd appreciate it if you saved me a plate."

"I can do that, *sohn*. When will you be back?"

"I'm not sure."

"I've heard Bailey Miller is back in the community."

"What?" He abandoned his task and poked his head into the kitchen. "What do you mean?"

"I guess she's helping out at the store while her *mamm* is laid up."

"Laid up?"

"Not literally. She's tending to a new *boppli*."

"*Ach.* That's right. Silas and Kayla just had another *bu, ain't not*?"

"*Jah.*"

"She's engaged, you know." He shook his head. "I lost my chance with her."

"It *chust* wasn't meant to be."

Timothy felt his ire rising. "You mean that you and *Daed* didn't want it to be. Because it *would* have been, if I'd had my way."

"MaryAnn was a nice *maedel*."

Timothy's hands balled into fists. "I didn't love her. Bailey's the *only* girl I've ever wanted for a *fraa*. And I think you know that."

"You never could forget her."

"How could I? Why would I?"

Mamm stared pointedly at him. "You know we didn't approve."

"*Jah*, I know. But I'm no longer seeking your approval. My life mate should be *my* decision. I am the one who will have to live with the one I marry."

"True."

"At this rate, I'll likely remain a bachelor my entire life. Because I couldn't bear marrying anyone but Bailey Miller. I love her as much today as I did when we were seventeen. I just wish I still had a chance with her."

"But you said she *wasn't* married yet, right?"

"Are you *encouraging* me to pursue a relationship with Bailey? Now? When she's promised to another man?"

"You're of age now, Timothy, and able to make up your own mind," *Mamm* said.

Unbelievable.

"Honestly, I'd rather see you happily married to Bailey Miller than a sad lonely old bachelor your whole life."

Wow. "Well, it looks to me that Bailey's already made her choice. And it's not me."

"*Der Herr's* will shall be done, *mei sohn.*"

"I suppose it will." He turned back to the task at hand, found Bailey's community and flipped to the P section. And there it was. Mark Petersheim's name and birthdate listed under his *vatter* and mother's name, along with his siblings. Timothy quickly jotted down the address.

An hour later, Timothy found himself driving by the Petersheims' place. He wasn't even sure what he would say to this Mark fellow, but he knew he had to say something.

I hope you know what a gem you're getting with Bailey Miller. Please be kind to her and love her with all your heart. Give her everything you can, because she's worth far more than anything you could ever give her.

Timothy stopped, shoving away a tear.

And if you decide between now and your wedding day, that you don't want to marry her, please let me know. Or maybe just send her back to me. Because I do love her with all my heart, and I think I will until the day I die. So if there is any shred of doubt in your mind of your love for her, please don't marry her. She deserves nothing less than to be loved. Cherish each day you have with her.

Ach. This was going to be even more difficult than he'd anticipated. How would he ever get through this conversation with his wits about him?

He pulled into the driveway, sighed, and stepped down from the buggy.

SEVEN

*B*ailey lifted the note from the back door of the store, reading it as she pulled out the key *Mamm* had given her last week. *Bailey, I have an appointment today and won't get to the store until mid-morning. Please get started on the list I left. I'll be there as soon as I can. - Jenny*

Appointment? Was *Aenti* Jenny expecting again? Bailey pushed the happy thought aside. There was work to be done.

The moment she entered the store, warmth immediately enveloped her. She'd never been so thankful for Silas's forethought. She'd forgotten how he would continually come and turn on the propane heaters prior to the store's opening. Her step*vatter* had always been helpful like that. *Jah,*

Mamm had married a *gut* one. Even if he hadn't been her biological *vatter*.

It seemed like every day was colder than the one before lately. Surely the snow would be arriving soon. A chill raced through her just thinking about it.

She removed her outer bonnet and placed it on the small table near the back door, but opted to keep her coat on for now.

She moved to the fridge, where *Aenti* Jenny always kept their checklist, and read through it. She stopped and bowed her head. They usually started the day with prayer—prayer for their family, prayer for their workday to run smoothly, and prayer that they would be a beacon of *Gott's* love to the community. Bailey added in an extra prayer for her current emotional state.

Now, to start on the bread dough.

Bailey pulled several loaves of bread from the oven and set them on the cooling racks. She smiled in satisfaction. Not only did it smell *wunderbaar* in the store, but her loaves had turned out perfectly. Unlike the last time she'd attempted to make bread in Nora's oven.

She'd made several batches of doughnuts and the case was now half-stocked. Cookies baked in the oven. The cinnamon rolls were well on their way to completion. She'd checked out four customers, and the day was still young.

When had the last time been that she'd felt so accomplished? She missed this feeling of usefulness. Not that she did nothing at *Dat* and Nora's. She did stuff. Mostly it was keeping the *kinner* occupied with learning games and projects or helping with meals and household tasks. Not that she didn't enjoy that too. It was just a different level of accomplishment than this was. Running a store and bakery by herself told her she was capable. She was intelligent. She was independent.

Bailey glanced out the window when something caught her eye. It was someone in a buggy. *Ach*, maybe it was Emily. Bailey had written in her last letter that she planned on working at the store this week. But she just sent it off on Saturday. Surely Emily wouldn't have received it yet. But it was possible she'd heard from one of her *brieder*, Silas or *Onkel* Paul, especially if they'd visited yesterday during their off-church week.

The bell above the door jingled and Bailey quickly cleaned her hands, then went to meet her visitor...or customer.

"*Ach*, it smells *wunderbaar* in here."

She'd know that voice anywhere. *Timothy*.

"Hi, Bailey." He looked around, as though searching for something. "Is your aunt here?"

"*Nee*, it's just me right now. But she'll be in later."

"Great. Can we talk?"

She shook her head. Her guard immediately rising. "Timothy, I don't think that's a *gut* idea."

He held up a hand. "It's important. I wouldn't have come here to see you if it wasn't. It's about Mark Petersheim."

Alarm rose in her chest. "What about Mark? Is he okay?"

76

Timothy eyed his former sweetheart. How he hated seeing the worry on her brow. He wished he could kiss it away. But she wasn't his. And he'd do *gut* to remind himself of that fact.

"*Jah*, he's fine. It's nothing like that"

She planted a hand on her hip. "Then what is it?"

"Bailey..." He sighed. "I don't want you to marry him."

"I already know that, Timothy. Too bad."

Her words felt like a knife in his heart, but he ignored them and continued with his mission. "If you're doing this to spite me, then please don't."

She gasped. "Wow, you must really think a lot of yourself."

"No, I don't." He hung his head.

"In spite of what you think, Timothy, my world does not revolve around you. Maybe it once did when I was younger and more naïve, but I'm not that girl anymore."

"Bailey, please. Could you just trust me?"

"Tried that before. Didn't work, remember?"

"Bailey, just..." *Ach*, she could be maddening

sometimes. "Mark's not a good man."

"I can't believe this." She pointed a finger at his chest. "Don't you dare, Timothy."

"Honest. I saw him at his job site. He lost his temper and flew off the handle. He even used words you would never *think* to say."

Her arms fastened across her chest. "What did you say to him, Timothy?"

"Me? I didn't say anything to him. I just witnessed a confrontation between him and another man."

"I don't see it as a big deal." She shrugged. "Everyone gets upset once in a while. Even *you*."

"I would never think to speak to someone the way he spoke to that man. And I'm not trying to be self-righteous or anything. I just hate to see you, of all people, saddled with someone like that for the rest of your life."

"So you want to be the hero and swoop in on your white horse to save me."

"Even if we never see each other again, I wouldn't want you to marry this Mark fellow. He's not for you, Bailey. You deserve better." His hands clenched together. "Will you *please* just listen to me? I care about you."

She stared at him. "Wait a minute. What were *you* doing at Mark's work?"

"I just...I had to go and see, Bailey. I wanted to meet this guy. I wanted to be sure he was good enough for you." He frowned. "Seems I got my answer without even speaking to him."

Her ire seemed to have melted away, and a smile threatened. "Just what did you plan on saying to him?"

He shrugged. "I never got that far. I was just going to say whatever came to mind."

Something akin to amusement danced in her eyes. "What? Like 'Hi, I'm Bailey's ex-beau. I just wanted to make sure you were good enough for her'?"

He couldn't help smiling. "Something like that."

A beautiful smile finally broke across her face and it took everything in him not to reach out and caress her cheek—or pull her into his arms.

Why had he been so foolish to let her go? Why

hadn't he stood up to his parents and insist on courting Bailey? It would have been wrong to defy them, but it felt more wrong now. How was he going to move on with his life if Bailey actually married this Mark guy? It would be his own fault. He drove her into the arms of another man. He'd likely be fraught with worry and fearing for her safety if they got hitched.

If he hadn't jumped to conclusions, Bailey and *he* would probably already have been married by now. His heart ached just thinking about all he'd forfeited because of silly rumors that turned out to be untrue. If only he could go back and have a do-over. If only Bailey would give him another chance.

He'd better leave while he was ahead. "Uh, I should go now. But I want to take one of those custard doughnuts."

"Help yourself."

Right. It was self-serve. He took the tongs and placed a doughnut into one of the small paper bags stacked near the doughnut case.

He moved to the counter and reached for his wallet.

She held up her hand. "No charge. It's on the house."

His heart warmed. "You're not mad at me?"

She moved her thumb and forefinger close together. "Maybe just a little bit." She smiled.

"*Gut.*" He winked, then stepped out the door, all the while praising *Gott* for His goodness.

Not only were he and Bailey on speaking terms again, but it seemed like they'd just gained something he'd thought they had lost forever.

Friendship.

Bailey watched longingly as Timothy hopped into his buggy and maneuvered his horse out of the small parking area and onto the road. She saw him lift his hand as he drove off. Taking a piece of her heart with him. Of course, Timothy had always owned a piece of her heart.

Why hadn't she feel this way when Mark drove off the other evening? Or at other times?

Had *Der Herr* just given her His answer? Or were her own feelings getting in the way?

She turned when she heard a noise from the back.

Her aunt Jenny emerged from behind the wall separating the back room from the baking area. "I'm sorry, Bailey. I didn't mean to listen in. I'd just slipped through the back door and I didn't want to interrupt. And, well, I overheard some of your conversation."

Bailey frowned. "Which part?"

"What Timothy said about Mark." Worried darkened her aunt's features. "Bailey, I want you to take him seriously. If Mark really is as Timothy says, you don't want to be tied to him for life. Please, just trust me on this one."

"But I've never seen Mark act out like that."

Jenny sighed. "Do you remember when I first came here? When I first met your *onkel* Paul?"

"*Jah.*"

"I was on the run from an abusive beau. When we were alone, he would treat me poorly. I knew that if I didn't get away, he'd end up killing me."

Bailey's eyes widened. "I never knew."

"Well, you were still young. But anyhow,

nobody knew Atlee was that way except for me. And when I mentioned something, nobody would believe it because he seemed like such a great guy to everybody else. I suffered quite a bit. I can only imagine the nightmare I'd be living if I were still with him." She shuddered.

"But Mark's never been that way with me."

"Chances are, he's on his best behavior since you're only courting. That could change the moment you take your vows, then do something he disapproves of. At that point, you would be stuck in a nightmare."

"I see what you're saying." Bailey rubbed her forehead. "But what if it was just a one-time thing with the guy at work? I don't want to base my assumption on what someone said—on rumors." Wasn't that what Timothy had done?

"Do you think Timothy would lie to you?"

"It wouldn't be the first time." But he had seemed sincere. And concerned. For her.

"Well, then, why don't you ask Mark about it? You should be able to tell from his reaction." She shrugged. "If you can't, then what about talking to his co-workers?"

"I don't know about talking to people behind his back. That feels a little devious. I don't want him to think I don't trust him. Because, other than Timothy's accusations, there really isn't a case."

"Well, why don't you just ask Mark about it then? And it wouldn't hurt to pray."

"I can do that." Bailey sighed, dreading even the thought of bringing up the subject to Mark. Fortunately, she wouldn't have to tackle that beast for another week. Until then, she'd let thoughts of Mark slip to the back of her mind, and enjoy her time in her *mamm's* Amish district.

EIGHT

Timothy had been quite busy lately, so it had been a couple of weeks since he last visited *Mammi* Stoltzfoos. But the holidays were nearing, and he figured it would be a *gut* time to stop in and say hello. *Mammi* had changed since she'd lost *Dawdi* earlier this year. She didn't smile as much as she used to, which was understandable. But each time Timothy saw *Mammi*, his heart went out to her.

Mammi and *Dawdi* had moved into Timothy's folks' *dawdi haus* just a few years ago. Until then, they'd lived on their own property. But since they were getting up in years, Timothy's *vatter* insisted his folks move into the small dwelling connected to their family's main home.

They hadn't protested much and Timothy believed it was because they cherished the thought of being next door to their *kinskinner*.

Their entire family enjoyed having their grandparents close by. When *Grossdawdi* Stoltzfoos passed away, it affected all of them. But this would be the first time in the last fifty-seven years that *Mammi* would be facing the holiday season without him. Timothy couldn't imagine being married to someone for that length of time and then suddenly losing them. Just the thought caused his heart to ache with grief. Especially when he considered that loved one could be Bailey Miller.

"*Kumm* in, Timothy," his *Mammi's* voice echoed through the door.

Timothy entered quickly to minimize the chill. "How did you know it was me?"

"You're due for a visit, and you always knock two times."

"I do?"

She nodded. "*Kumm* and let your old *grossmammi* see you."

He moved closer and took her outstretched hand.

"Yep. Still look like your handsome *Grossdawdi*. He was about your age when we married." Her eyes took on a faraway look.

"How old was he?"

"We married young. Twenty-one. We both were."

"Same age as me."

"Any plans?"

"To marry?" He shook his head. *If only...* "*Nee.*"

"That's too bad. I'd think a handsome boy like you would have been snatched up by now."

He wouldn't tell her about his and Bailey's plans back in the day. But it didn't matter now. He'd blown that chance. Big time. "*Gott's* timing is perfect."

"Tell me what you've been up to." She gestured to the rocker across from her own and he took a seat.

"I got involved in a project at the library. I ran into Bailey Miller there." Now why had he gone and mentioned Bailey? Likely because he couldn't seem to get her out of his head lately.

"Your *grossdawdi* always thought you and the Miller *maedel* made a *gut* couple."

Timothy frowned. "How did you know we used to date?"

"Don't you remember? You brought her over one time. What was it, nigh unto four or five years ago, if I remember correctly."

"I did?"

"*Jah*. She helped me make cookies. A sweet *maedel*, she was."

"Ah, cookies. *Now* I remember."

His *grossmammi* chuckled. "*Chust* like a boy, always excited about something when it involves food."

Pulling a smile from her lips made Timothy's heart glad. It had been missing more often than not lately.

"Your *grossdawdi* had gone on and on about the Miller girl. Is she married now, then?"

"*Ach, nee*. Not yet. Engaged, I think."

"But not to you?"

"*Nee.*" He frowned.

"That's too bad. We were sure and certain the two of you would get hitched."

"She lives in another district now, with her *vatter.*"

"I see. But you ran into her at the library?" She stared toward the wall calendar. "I always liked that old library. Checked out many a book from there. Your *grossdawdi* always liked the old western novels."

Timothy smiled. "I never knew that *Dawdi* liked to read."

"We both enjoyed reading. *Ach,* how I miss him."

Timothy noticed his *grossmammi's* eyes misting. He leaned forward and covered one of her hands with his. "I bet it's hard."

Her shaky hand wiped away a tear. "I always hoped I'd go first, but *Der Herr* must've known better."

"I think it's amazing that you had over fifty years together."

"I suppose I should be grateful for the time *Der*

Herr gave us together, but it's hard living life without the one you've loved for so many years. When they're gone, you *chust* want to go too."

His brow furrowed. "I reckon grief is a part of the healing process, but I wish I knew a way to make it easier for you."

"Don't you go worrying over your *Mammi*. I'll be fine. *Der Herr* will get me through."

"Is there anything I can do for you, *Mammi*?"

"Not that I can think of. Unless you want to bring in a bit more kindling."

"I can do that." Timothy moved toward the door.

"What am I thinking, *chust* sitting here chewing the fat?" She sprung up from her rocker. "What kind of a *grossmammi* am I if I don't offer this *bu* something to eat."

"That's okay, *Mammi*. I'm not really hungry."

She waved a hand in front of her face. "Pff. Nonsense. *Buwe* are always hungry."

Ten minutes later, Timothy was sitting at the table with a large plate of dippy eggs, toast, bacon, and a cup of orange juice.

He smiled. In spite of her own grief, she found pleasure in serving others. You just had to love grandmothers.

NINE

Bailey frowned when Friday rolled around. Aside from his visit on Monday to warn her about Mark, Timothy hadn't stopped by the store. She didn't understand why she was disappointed. It wasn't like the two of them had a future together. Truly, she shouldn't even be thinking about him at all. But she couldn't help it. The fact that Timothy entered her mind more often than Mark, the man she would be marrying, was plain wrong.

I probably won't even miss you.

Why, of all the things Mark had said to her, did *those* words seem to linger? Why couldn't something *positive* about him be stuck in her head instead? She closed her eyes, attempting to recall *gut* things about Mark. But her brain must have been in a fog. Because, for the life of her, all she could think of was Mark talking about work and money and what he was going to buy next. She thought of his reaction to her little half-brother Noah, when he'd reached his arms to Mark and asked him to hold him. Timothy would have swooped the little one up in a heartbeat. *That* she knew for a fact.

And there she went, comparing Mark and Timothy to each other. Again.

"Bailey, you're coming back next week, right?"

Aenti Jenny's voice distracted her thoughts. A *gut* thing. "*Jah*. Monday, Tuesday, and Wednesday. Do you need me here on Friday too?"

"*Nee*, I don't think so. I was going to talk to your *mamm* about staying closed on Thursday and Friday. I want to go shopping on Friday when they have all the *gut* deals. You're welcome to come along, if you'd like."

She thought about the shoebox gifts she still needed to buy. "Let me talk to *Dat* and Nora. I think I'd like to come along."

"Oh, *gut*. And if you know of anyone else who might like to come, you're welcome to invite them as well."

She thought of Timothy. Had he already purchased the gifts for his boxes?

As though he'd read her mind, Timothy rushed through the entrance of the store. "Oh, *gut*! You're still here, Bailey. I was hoping you'd help me with something before you go back home."

Why did her heart just flip flop? "Timothy, I—"

"Before you say no, just hear me out, please."

"I wasn't going to say no."

"You weren't?" His grin stretched across his face.

Why did he have to have such an attractive smile? *Ach*, she shouldn't be thinking about his smile. *Bad, Bailey.*

"I'm not saying yes *yet*." She couldn't suppress her own grin. She flicked a glance at *Aenti* Jenny, who pretended not to be listening. "What I meant was, what is it?"

Taking the hint, her aunt disappeared into the back room.

"It's two things, actually." He chuckled. "I'm greedy, aren't I?"

Ach, Timothy was the least greedy person she knew.

"Depends on what you want," she teased. Her teeth momentarily held her bottom lip captive.

"Well, first, I wanted to tell you that our boxes need to be in by next week."

"Are yours filled already?"

"I have stuff for a couple, but I plan on doing more because we didn't get as many volunteers as I'd hoped."

Bailey frowned. She wouldn't tell him that she'd asked Mark and he'd said no.

"I could probably fill two, then. I've made a little money working at the store this week."

"I won't ask you to, but you can if you'd like. Don't you need to buy gifts for your family too?"

"I do. But I'm probably going to be working here through Christmas, maybe longer. I'll have enough saved up by then to buy gifts for everyone."

"You're amazing, Bailey." He suddenly reddened. "I mean—"

"So are you." *Ach*! Now why had she gone and said that?

She didn't miss the yearning look in his eyes.

"Bailey, I—"

What was she doing? "The second thing you wanted to ask about?" She recovered.

"*Jah*." He shook his head. "The second thing. I was hoping you could help me with ideas for *mei mammi*."

"Your *mammi*?"

"*Jah*. She's been depressed since *mei dawdi* died earlier this year. I want to do something for her that would cheer her up. She puts on a brave face, but I know she's really struggling. Says she wishes she could be with *Grossdawdi*." Tears shimmered in Timothy's eyes. "I don't want to lose her too."

Bailey felt moisture pooling in her own eyes. She covered his hand with hers. "I'm sorry, Timothy."

Ever since she'd broken through his rough exterior back when they were in school, she'd learned that deep down, Timothy Stoltzfoos had a sensitive side. He didn't show it often, but when he did, it had always pulled at Bailey's heartstrings. Timothy genuinely cared for others. *Nee*, he wasn't greedy at all. He was quite perfect.

"Yes," she blurted out.

"Yes, what?"

"To helping your *mammi*. I think I might have some ideas."

"I was actually on my way to the library right now." He glanced outside.

That was when Bailey noticed a driver waiting out in the car for him. "Oh. Well, if you need to go..."

"I was hoping you'd come with me." His words rushed out. "There's something at the library I'd really like to show you. It's about the shoeboxes."

Bailey frowned. "*Ach*, I need to help *Aenti* Jenny close up the store. We still have an hour yet."

"Go ahead, Bailey." Her aunt said as she stepped around the back partition. "I've closed by myself plenty of times. I'll be fine."

Bailey blinked. "You're sure?"

"*Jah*, I'm sure and certain." A knowing look

flashed across her aunt's face. Although, Bailey didn't know exactly what it meant.

"*Geh*. With. Timothy." *Aenti* Jenny's head cocked toward the door, but Bailey got the feeling her aunt's statement implied more than just going to the library with Timothy.

"*Ach, jah*. Okay. If you're sure." Her gaze flitted to Timothy, whose eagerness couldn't seem to be tamped down.

"I'm sure." Her aunt smiled.

"Okay, just tell *Mamm* that I'll come back to get my buggy later, then."

"I'll do that." *Aenti* Jenny promised.

Timothy stood, ready to open the door. His intense gaze met hers. "You ready?"

In more ways than one, yes.

She nodded, then followed him out the door.

TEN

Timothy *had* to be stuck in a wonderful dream. That was the only logical explanation for his current circumstances.

He couldn't believe Bailey had agreed to go with him. He figured he'd ask her, but the possibility of her responding with a yes had seemed like a long shot. And now here they both were, in the same car, riding to the library.

He'd offered to let her sit in the front, but she'd opted for the back seat. He'd wanted to join her so badly he could taste it, but she might not think it was appropriate since she was seeing that Mark guy. He wondered whether she'd spoken to him about what Timothy had seen. He guessed not since he'd learned that she'd stayed at her *mamm's* all week. Unless she'd called and talked to him over the phone. He wouldn't ask, though, since it really was none of his business. Oh, but he'd like to make it his business. He'd like to give that Mark guy a good talking to.

Fortunately, their quiet ride to the library hadn't lasted long. He was often amazed how much quicker it was to get from point A to point B when a car was involved. He couldn't wait to be alone with Bailey again. The awkwardness when others were around was unnerving.

As soon as they entered the library, Timothy borrowed one of the laptops the library loaned out to patrons. He then beckoned Bailey to follow him to the lower level where they had allowed him to keep the shoebox project items.

He set the laptop down on one of the tables and powered the device on.

"Are these the boxes that have come in?" Bailey eyed the stacks under and on top of the table.

"*Jah*." He shrugged. "It's a decent amount, I guess. I'd hoped more people would volunteer."

"Don't be discouraged. Even one box would be

a blessing to someone."

"You're right." *Ach,* how he loved Bailey with everything in him. If only he could have a second chance with her.

"Bailey, come here. I want to show you something." Enthusiasm accompanied Timothy's words, as he beckoned her toward the computer in front of him.

"What is it?" She joined him at the computer, curious about why he was so excited.

He vacated the chair and gestured for her to sit.

She deliberated a moment. Should she really be getting comfortable with Timothy? She finally acquiesced and dropped into the chair.

Timothy squatted down beside the chair, then his focus returned to the screen. "See this?"

"What?" She looked at the children of different ethnicities on the screen, but had no clue what he was wanting her to see specifically.

"This is one of the places they've sent the shoeboxes to in the past. Look." He pointed to the screen.

Tears pricked her eyes as she viewed photo after photo of children opening shoeboxes similar to the ones she and Timothy were going to fill. "They look so happy."

Timothy touched something on the computer, and a short video of children opening their boxes began playing. The excited looks on their faces were priceless. They exhibited pure joy over the smallest things she took for granted.

"Read the messages. Especially this one."

"I loved all my gifts, but I was so happy to learn about Jesus. I asked Him to save me, and now, I am going to Heaven! Thank you for sending me love."

Bailey shook her head. "That's amazing!"

"Isn't it?" He pointed to the screen. "Read this one."

"Thank you for sending me my very own toothbrush! Now I don't need to share with the other ten girls in the unit we live in at our orphanage."

Moisture surfaced in Bailey's eyes. "Are they serious?"

Timothy frowned. "I'm afraid so."

"Wow. I just saw a pack of five toothbrushes at the dollar store. Maybe we should buy several of those packs."

Timothy shrugged. "We could, but we have no idea who they're going to. It might not be an orphanage."

"Still. Don't you think they would need toothbrushes?"

"I suppose it wouldn't hurt to send along extras."

"Do you think they share other personal items as well? Like brushes and combs?" Bailey voiced her thoughts.

"I would imagine so."

"Don't you just wish you could help all of them?"

"*Jah*." He shrugged. "But like you said. Just one will make a difference in someone's life. And we're sending in all of those." He pointed to their filled shoeboxes near the table beside them.

"*Ach*, I'm so excited about all of this." She turned from the screen and stared at him. "I just had an idea."

Jennifer Spredemann

"About what?"

"Your *mammi*. What if we get her involved in this?"

"How?"

"Well, we could tell her about the project—"

"*Ach*! We can *show* her. I can borrow this laptop from the library. I think the battery will last at least a couple of hours. It'll only take maybe thirty minutes if she wants to read over the information on the website."

Bailey nodded. "That's a *gut* idea. I was thinking that we could maybe take her shopping with us to purchase items for our boxes. And she can help wrap the boxes too."

"I'm so glad you thought of that, Bailey. I know that when we take our eyes off our own hurt and focus on someone else in need, our own pain lessens and we feel better knowing we've helped someone else. Hopefully, *Mammi* will feel the same way."

"Exactly."

"Well, what are we waiting for?" He stood, but stopped in his tracks. "Or, can you *kumm* see

Mammi right now?"

"I guess I could go for just a little bit, but my *dat* is expecting me home before too long. I can call from your phone shanty and let him know I'll be a little late."

"*Wunderbaar.*" He looked like he wanted to hug her. She felt like she wanted to hug him.

With his handsome smile, and the twinkle in his eye, she felt like they were seventeen all over again. When was the last time she'd felt this *gut* about something?

She knew. It was when she found out, at the age of seventeen, that her *vatter* was alive after believing he was dead all those years.

ELEVEN

Timothy really needed to pinch himself so he'd awaken from his dream, because continuing on like this was not healthy for his heart in the least. But he didn't want to wake up. It was too *wunderbaar*. He wanted to stay in this dream forever.

Him and Bailey. Together. Laughing. Teasing. Planning.

Just a week ago, she'd been giving him what for at the library. And he'd deserved every bit of it. He didn't deserve a second chance with her. But something was happening between them. And he knew that Bailey felt it too. And in spite of her relationship with her "almost fiancé," she hadn't tried to stop this growing relationship between the two of them. Timothy had a feeling she was enjoying their time together almost as much as he was. The thought thrilled his heart like nothing else.

But if he had to lose her all over again...

"Is your *grossmammi* expecting us?"

Bailey's words from the backseat of his driver's car reminded him this was indeed *real* and not a dream.

The driver let them out in front of the *dawdi haus*, as Timothy instructed, and Timothy quickly paid him.

He turned to Bailey. "*Nee*. But she'll love to see you. She went on and on about you the other day."

A beautiful smile graced her lips. *Ach*, how he longed to pull her into his arms and kiss her like he had when they were courting. But as long as she belonged to someone else, it wasn't his right. He had to respect her choice. Because she hadn't chosen him. Not this time.

"How sweet is that."

Not as sweet as you.

They would visit with his *mammi,* then the two of them would ride back to Bailey's *mamm's* house, where her buggy was. They'd be in his courting buggy again. Alone. Together. Just like old times.

"Are you ready to go in?" He held the laptop under one of his arms.

Bailey nodded and he knocked on the door. Twice. So *Mammi* would know it was him.

"*Kumm* in, Timothy." *Mammi's* voice called from inside. He knew that when she didn't physically answer the door, she was likely in her hickory rocker working on one of her word find puzzles she seemed to have become addicted to. Prior to Grossdawdi's passing, it had been a crochet project.

Bailey gasped. "How does she know it's you?"

"Two knocks. Apparently, I'm the only one who knocks that way." He shrugged, then opened the door.

"You go first," Bailey whispered.

He nodded. "Guess what, *Mammi*? I brought somebody with me." He grinned like a fool.

"Now, how can I guess when you *chust* told me the answer? There's no fun in that." *Mammi* set her word puzzle to the side.

He motioned for Bailey to step forward. "*Mammi*, you remember Bailey, right?"

"*Jah*. Of course, I remember her. Especially since we were *chust* talking about her on Monday."

Bailey's brow quirked and a sudden rush of warmth filled Timothy's face.

He cleared his throat. "*Jah, vell*, I talked her into coming to see you."

"Talked her into it?" *Mammi* tsked.

"Well, no, not really." Timothy fumbled over his words.

Bailey spoke up, "What he *means* to say is I *wanted* to come see you. I haven't seen you in a long time. How have you been?"

Ach, how he loved this woman.

"I've seen better days." *Mammi* sighed, the sides of her mouth pulling downward.

Bailey moved close to *Mammi's* chair and enveloped Timothy's *grossmammi* in an embrace.

"I'm really sorry about John. I bet it's difficult for you."

When Bailey moved back, Timothy noticed both she and *Mammi* had tears in their eyes.

He and Bailey both found a seat. He knew that if *Mammi* were her usual self, she'd immediately offer them refreshments of some kind.

Mammi's shaky hand whisked away a few tears. "When you've been married to someone nearly sixty years, you tend to miss them when they're gone. His place next to me is empty in the morning, and I know it isn't *chust* because he went to feed the calves. His place at the head of the table is empty, his seat is vacant every day. He's no longer here to tell my stories to, to laugh when I say crazy things, or to pray with me when I am worried or down. And when I slip into bed at night, his place is still cold and empty. I can no longer reach out and touch him, run my fingers through his hair. Hear him protest when I put my cold feet on him."

Tears were now running down all three of their faces. Timothy had never heard his *grossmammi* open up this much.

Mammi continued, "You know, it's the little things I miss the most. Like *chust* sitting quietly in the *schtupp* in the evening while I crochet and he reads the paper. Now, I can't even crochet. It's like I've forgotten who I am without him."

Bailey reached out and covered *Mammi's* hand with her own.

"I don't know how I'll be able to get through the holidays. John and I never had any grand celebrations, but he always gave me a small simple gift to let me know he cared."

Now was the time. Timothy looked to Bailey, his brow raised. She nodded and gestured toward the laptop, which now rested on his legs.

"Speaking of gifts. Did Timothy tell you what we're doing this year?" Bailey forged on.

Mammi shook her head. "What are you doing?"

"Well, there's this organization that asks for people to volunteer. And what we do is, we get an empty shoebox—"

"Or a person could buy a plastic one," Timothy added. He powered up the computer.

Bailey continued, "And we wrap it up in fancy Christmas paper. Then we fill it up with gifts and other things people might need, like toothbrushes and such. And then the organization comes by and picks up the shoeboxes that the volunteers filled up, and they deliver them to needy people in poor countries."

"Let me show you." He held the laptop in front of *Mammi*, pushed Play, and the video began.

Mammi's gaze was riveted on the screen. "*Ach,* this is *wunderbaar!*" A spark lit her eyes.

"We were hoping you could help us fill up some shoeboxes." Bailey smiled. "Would you like to help?"

"Where are they picking these boxes up from?" *Mammi* stared at Timothy.

"The library. That's why I was there the other day. And where I ran into Bailey."

"I see." *Mammi* nodded.

"We were hoping you would come shopping with us next week, so we can buy items to fill up the boxes," Bailey added.

"You..." *Mammi* stared at Bailey, then looked

to him. "And Timothy?"

Bailey nodded. "Well, *jah*. I mean, if *you're* coming along. We'll just hire a driver and go into Madison. Probably the dollar store and Walmart."

"I suppose I could use a few things from Walmart."

"Great!" Timothy grinned.

"Now, I think it's time I fixed you two something to eat." With a burst of what seemed like renewed energy, *Mammi* sprung up from her chair.

Timothy hated to dampen her joy, but... "*Mammi*, I need to take Bailey back to her *mamm's* so she can drive home before it gets too dark."

Bailey put a hand on his forearm and shook her head. "It's okay, Timothy. If it gets too late, I may just call *Dat* and tell him I'm spending the night at *Mamm's* again."

"*Ach*, really? You're sure?"

She gestured her head toward his *grossmammi*, and mouthed, "she's lonely" while *Mammi's* back was turned.

He nodded, unable to conceal his grin. "Bring it on, *Mammi*. It looks like we're staying."

TWELVE

What on earth are you doing, Bailey? She chided herself.

Spending all this time with Timothy was not a wise idea in the least. But she couldn't just leave his poor *grossmammi* by herself. Especially after she'd poured out her heart to the two of them. It was like they'd established a special connection. A connection of the heart.

Bailey wished they already had all their Christmas items, so they could begin wrapping and packaging right now. Because she was sure if they did, Timothy's *grossmammi's* spirits would lift even more.

Which sparked an idea.

She moved to the kitchen, where his

grossmammi had gone, and Timothy followed.

"Do you have the ingredients for cookies?" she asked his *grossmammi*. "If so, we could make some. Even Timothy could help." And there she went, flirting with Timothy again.

"So you want to wrangle me into women's work, huh?"

Mammi tossed him an apron. "Man up."

Bailey laughed when a worried look flashed over Timothy's face. "Sounds like you better listen to your *grossmammi*. Who knows? You might just find that you enjoy women's work."

"Ha. Ha." Timothy rolled his eyes, but donned the apron nonetheless. He glanced down at the frilly polka dot garment and pointed at Bailey. "You're *going* to pay for this. You know that, right?"

"If I only had a camera!" Bailey laughed.

He glanced toward his *grossmammi*, who grinned. By the pleased look on Timothy's face, Bailey guessed he'd wear the apron every day if it brought this much joy to his *grossmammi*. *Ach*, he was such a *gut*, caring *gross sohn*.

Did Mark ever do stuff like this for his *grossmammi*? *Stop it, Bailey!*

"Okay, so…chocolate chip cookies?" Timothy rubbed his hands together. "*Mammi*, do you have the stuff for them?"

"The ingredients, you mean." His *grossmammi* pulled a couple of plastic canisters out of the pantry and set them on the table. "Bailey, you can fetch the large mixing bowl out of the cupboard behind you."

She did as instructed.

"What can I do?" Timothy asked.

His *grossmammi* held up a wooden spoon. "Stay out of mischief."

"Is that a warning, *Mammi*?" Timothy chuckled.

Mammi glanced at the spoon in her hand and laughed. "No, but it could be. I believe I still know how to use this."

Ach, when was the last time Bailey had this much fun?

"You go wash your hands." *Mammi* aimed the wooden spoon at Timothy again.

"Yes, *Mammi*." Timothy saluted, then moved toward the kitchen sink.

His *grossmammi* swatted him on the rear end with her wooden spoon.

Timothy spun around. "Hey! What'd I do?"

"Didn't your *mamm* ever teach you not to wash your filthy hands where we put the dishes that we eat off of?"

"*Nee*. And my hands aren't really filthy."

"*Ach*, what is this world coming to?" *Mammi* raised her hands, then pointed toward the back door. "To the mud room. Now."

Timothy turned and looked at Bailey, a half-worried grimace on his face. "That's not a substitute for the woodshed, is it?"

His *grossmammi* laughed. "*Nee, dummkopp*. It's where you wash your hands."

Bailey couldn't help laughing out loud. Nor could she help the tears running down her face.

Timothy returned, holding up freshly washed hands. "I'm so glad I can provide entertainment for you two. Now, what's next?"

"The measuring cups and spoons are in that

drawer." *Mammi* pointed, then returned to the pantry. She handed a bag of semi-sweet chocolate chips to Bailey. "I'm giving them to you because I don't trust him with them."

"I have a distinct feeling I'm being picked on tonight." Timothy protested. "Contrary to popular opinion, I can occasionally behave myself."

"*Occasionally* about sums it up. I saw all the mischief you and your *brieder* used to get into. And if I remember correctly, you were the ringleader." *Mammi* stared at him.

"You should have seen him at school," Bailey added her two cents.

"I can only imagine." *Mammi* shook her head. She pointed to Timothy. "You. Plant yourself down right there." She gestured to the bench at the table. "Now, can we trust you to measure out the ingredients correctly?"

Bailey pressed her lips together to hold in a giggle.

"*Ach, Mammi.* I'm not one of the *kinner* anymore," Timothy complained.

After *Mammi* and Bailey set all of the ingredients on the table, Bailey sat across the way from Timothy.

"Now, this old *maedel* is going to go prop her feet up. I expect to have some cookies finished in no less than twenty minutes." She aimed her gaze at Timothy. "Do you understand?"

"Yes, *Mammi*."

His *grossmammi* turned to Bailey, thrusting the wooden spoon into her hand. "And I'm counting on *you* to keep him in line."

"I'll do my best." Bailey smiled.

As soon as they heard his *grossmammi* sit down in the other room, Bailey leaned forward and whispered, "I think it's working."

"What's working?" Timothy whispered back across the table.

"Our plan to cheer up your *grossmammi*."

"I think you're right." He leaned forward. "And why are we whispering?"

"We don't want her to know we're scheming."

"We are?"

Bailey giggled. "You."

"Me? What about me?"

"I think you exasperate your *mammi* sometimes."

He shrugged. "I have no idea why."

"It's awfully quiet in there," *Mammi's* voice drifted from the living room. "Timothy James Stoltzfoos, there's no hanky-panky going on in there, *ain't not*?"

"*Nee, Mammi*. Bailey and I are just talking quietly," he replied.

"Twenty minutes," she hollered back.

"Right." Timothy smiled at Bailey. "It looks like we better start mixing some cookie dough."

Timothy wished this evening would never end.

His *grossmammi* should be satisfied that they'd just put the final batch of cookies into the oven.

Timothy reached into the bag of leftover chocolate chips. "Here, open your mouth." He held a chocolate chip in his hand to toss it to her.

Bailey shook her head.

"Ah, come on." He handed her a chocolate chip. "Here, you shoot first." He stepped back and opened his mouth.

Bailey look unsure, but she tossed it anyway.

The chocolate chip landed squarely on his cheek. He chuckled. "Almost. Try again."

"You ready?"

"Go for it." He squatted down slightly, opening his mouth.

She threw the chocolate chip. It bounced off his nose and into his mouth.

He laughed. "Hey, that was pretty *gut*. Got some backboard in there."

She giggled. "I wasn't aiming for the backboard."

"Okay, let me try now."

She tugged in her lip. *Gut*. She was contemplating it. "Okay, I guess. But I'm closing my eyes."

"I better be a decent shot then." He grabbed a chocolate chip. "Ready?"

She nodded, then closed her eyes.

He took a second to study how beautiful she was. And how happy and comfortable she seemed with him right now.

"Okay. Here it comes." He tossed the chocolate chip.

It sailed through the air, pinged off her tooth, then went into her mouth.

"I did it." He laughed.

"I'm just glad you didn't break my tooth."

"Nah, only chipped it."

"What?" She thrust a hand to her mouth, feeling her tooth.

"Get it? Chipped? As in chocolate chips?"

She shook her head. "You." Her finger pointed at his chest.

He was tempted to grasp her finger and pull her into his arms. Instead, he did the first thing he could think of. He reached into the canister and grasped a pinch of flour. "Stand back. I'm armed."

He held up his two fingers pinching the flour.

Bailey giggled. "You wouldn't."

"Oh ho. Don't ever dare me. That's dangerous ground right there."

She thrust a hand on her hip. "I know you wouldn't. Not in your *grossmammi's* kitchen," she challenged.

He glanced back to make sure *Mammi* wasn't standing behind him. He took a step closer.

"Wouldn't I?"

"You better not."

Ach, but he'd never backed down from a challenge. And this one was just too fun to resist.

In two quick steps toward her, he released the flour over her head.

Her mouth opened in pure astonishment as the particles of flour floated down her face and the front of her cape.

"Timothy James Stoltzfoos! I can't believe you just did that to this poor *maedel*." A voice came from behind.

Oh no. *Mammi*.

Just then, the timer sounded.

"Saved by the bell!" Timothy spun around, grasped a pot holder, and removed two trays of treats from the oven. "Cookies, anyone?"

"Why, yes. I do believe *Bailey and I* will go into the other room and enjoy some cookies. While *you* clean up this kitchen." She locked arms with Bailey. "What do you say?"

She giggled. "That sounds like a plan to me."

Timothy grunted.

And just like that, he was left in the kitchen. Alone.

But, oh, the ride home!

THIRTEEN

Bailey closed her eyes, enjoying the clip clop of the horse's hooves. Enjoying the faint scent of Timothy's aftershave. Enjoying the nearness in his buggy, as they shared one of his *grossmammi's* quilts to fend off the night chill.

This was wrong in so many ways.

"You tired?"

Her eyes opened and she glanced at Timothy. "*Nee*, not really. It's not that late."

"I'm sorry I kept you so long."

"You are?"

"Well, *nee*, not really. But if you should've been home..." He shrugged.

"No one's going to miss me." She frowned.

His brow arched. "No one? Really?"

"Probably not."

"What about Mark?"

She shook her head. "I doubt he misses me."

"What is *wrong* with that guy?"

"The thing is, I don't really miss him either. What's wrong with *me*?"

"It sounds like something's not clicking in that relationship."

"It's strange, isn't it?"

"*Nee*, not really. I think that maybe your attention is just focused on other things." His eyes flickered to her then back to the road.

Jah, her attention was definitely focused on *other* things. She should change the subject.

"Do you ever feel out of place? Like you don't belong anywhere?"

Timothy frowned, then turned to stare at her. "*Nee*. Do you?"

She looked toward the road to remind him that *he* was the one who should be watching it. She shrugged. "Sometimes, I guess."

"Why?"

"I don't know. It's just my *mamm* and Silas

have their family. And *Dat* and Nora have their family. I guess I kind of feel like a third wheel. Like I don't really belong."

"What about with Mark?"

"See. That's the thing. I don't really feel like I belong with him either. I don't know if I was thinking that maybe marrying him would change that. But I get the feeling it won't."

He reached over and squeezed her shoulder through the quilt. "You'll always belong in *Gott's* family, Bailey. You know that, right? He promised to never leave you nor forsake you."

"I know. But thanks for the reminder. I always find comfort when I read *Gott's* Word."

"How do you feel...do you feel you belong...with me?" He was back to staring again.

Her heart stuttered. "Honestly..." She stared down at the quilt. "I'm not ready for this conversation yet."

"Okay." He nodded. "I'll drop it, then."

"*Denki.*"

"Is Monday a *gut* time to go shopping for you?"

"After I get off work, *jah.*"

"Okay. What time should I have the driver pick you up?"

"Hmm...I hadn't thought of that. Because there's supper and all, and we'll likely be out for a while, *ain't not*?"

"How about if I treat you and *Mammi* to dinner out? As a thank you for helping me."

"I'm not doing the shoeboxes for you."

"*Ach, nee.* I know that. I meant for helping me with *Mammi*."

"You don't have to buy me dinner for that."

"Bailey." Frustration laced his tone. "Don't rob me of a blessing."

"What do you mean?"

"Well, I'm *trying* to do something nice for you and *Mammi*. Just...let me. *Please*."

Bailey noted the sincerity in his words. "*Jah*. Okay, then."

But it sounded a little too much like a date to her. With his *grossmammi* along, of course.

After Timothy tethered the horse to the hitching

post near the front of the house, he walked Bailey to the Millers' door.

She knocked on the door. "Isn't it weird that I knock on the door when I come here?"

"Not really. You don't live with Silas and Kayla anymore, so—"

Silas swung the door open. He smiled at Bailey, then his eyes shifted to Timothy. "Timothy Stoltzfoos." His eyebrow lifted. "Didn't expect to see you here. With Bailey." He looked to his stepdaughter for answers, stepping out of the and gesturing for them to enter.

"We were visiting with Timothy's *grossmammi*. And discussing the shoebox charity project," Bailey explained, as Silas closed the door behind them.

They removed their outerwear and placed it on the rack near the door.

Her step*vatter* eyed both of them curiously, zeroing in on Bailey's spotted white cape dress. "Did an explosion occur?" Amusement danced in Silas's eyes.

Bailey pointed at Timothy's chest. "It was all *his* fault."

Timothy grinned, holding up both of his hands. "Guilty as charged." He explained, "We were making cookies."

"Ah, I see."

Kayla called them further inside, a small bundle nestled in her arms.

Timothy smiled. "Is this the new one?"

Silas joined Kayla, moving the blanket from the *boppli's* face so he could be seen better. "This is the new one. Baby Caleb."

Ach, Timothy couldn't wait until *he* was the one celebrating the birth of a little one of his own. *Please let it be with Bailey as mei fraa, Gott.*

"Isn't he adorable?" Bailey now cradled the little one in her arms.

Timothy nodded, but all he could see was Bailey holding a *boppli* of their own making. *Ach*, he was in deep trouble!

"Why don't you two take a seat?" Kayla gestured toward the comfy living room couch.

Timothy swallowed. He and Bailey had *gut* memories on that couch. They hadn't shared their first kiss there, but many others. "*Jah*, okay." He nodded to Bailey, hoping she would lead the way.

He had already decided that if Bailey sat on the couch, he'd take one of the rocking chairs. No need to give anyone ideas. They weren't a couple. And he'd do *gut* to remind himself of that fact. Although he yearned for the opposite to be true.

By the time he got to the living room, all the vacant chairs had been taken by Bailey's folks and a couple of her siblings. Only a narrow spot between Bailey and the couches' arm remained. *Ach*, he was in trouble. He attempted to, as casually as possible, sink down beside Bailey.

The *boppli* made a noise, drawing Timothy's attention. He smiled down at the little one, really seeing him for the first time. The *boppli's* eyes were wide open and his tiny mouth looked like he was attempting to create sound. "You're a cute little guy." He stroked Caleb's tiny hand.

The *boppli's* gaze locked on him, and Timothy couldn't help but grin. "Yes, you are. Do you like it when your sister Bailey holds you?" He didn't care if he was speaking baby talk. Wasn't that what everyone did around babies?

"Yes, he does," Bailey cooed. "He loves his big sister. Doesn't he?"

They both admired the sweet thing, sharing a smile with each other.

When Timothy glanced up, he noticed both Silas and Kayla watching them. Silas lifted a brow then gestured toward the kitchen with his head. Why did Timothy's hands suddenly feel clammy?

He stood up and followed Silas to the kitchen. A couple of the *kinner* had followed, but Silas promptly instructed them to return to the living room.

"What's going on with you and Bailey?" Silas held his thumb behind one of his suspenders as he leaned against the counter, his gaze probing Timothy.

Great. Straightforward and to the point.

Timothy swallowed. "Nothing." His face may as well have been on fire, because he was certain he must be as red as the strawberries he grew in his greenhouse last summer.

"You sure about that?" Doubt laced Silas's words.

"She already has a beau. I know that."

"Yet you're *here*. And you've obviously been spending time with her."

Busted. "I have," he admitted.

"Look, Timothy. I don't have anything against you. But you left her broken." He pointed toward the living room. "And that will *never* happen again. Do you understand?"

Timothy didn't think Silas was trying to accentuate his muscles. It was just the natural occurrence of him simply crossing his arms. But for Timothy, it felt a bit intimidating. Not that he thought Silas would ever use force with him, or any man, for that matter.

"I understand."

"Do you love her?" Silas frowned.

"I do."

Silas sighed, squeezing his eyes closed.

"I don't think I ever stopped."

"I'm not sure if I agree with that," Silas challenged, now staring a hole through him.

"I know I was a *dummkopp*."

"You almost ruined her. At the least, she left

our district. She *could* have gone to the *Englisch* world. I don't think you realize what your actions nearly cost all of us."

"I don't know what to say."

"I'm not sure it's the best idea for the two of you to spend time together." Silas frowned, but his words may as well have been a serrated knife cutting through Timothy's heart.

"I'm afraid we're kind of already committed."

"You're *what*?"

"*Nee*, not to each other. To the Christmas shoebox project. We're working on it together. With *mei mammi*."

"When is the project complete?"

"We turn them in by the end of this week." The thought of not seeing Bailey after next week saddened him.

"*Gut*."

"I want to marry her," Timothy blurted out.

Silas shook his head. "As I recall, you told her that once before."

"Probably many times." Timothy couldn't help but smile.

"Does she feel the same way?"

"I don't know." Timothy grimaced. "But Mark isn't the right man for her."

"And *you* are?"

"I think so. She doesn't love Mark."

"Did she tell you this?"

Timothy shook his head. "In not so many words."

"You don't think you're reading too much into what she's *not* saying? Because I've seen her and Mark together. They make a *gut* couple. He's planning on building a house for them, already bought the property."

Timothy swallowed. What was he even doing here? Why did he think he had a chance with Bailey?

"I understand that you still care for her, Timothy. But you had your chance. And, honestly, I wish you wouldn't get involved with Bailey again. It took her a long time, but she has finally been able to move on after dealing with your heartbreak."

And there it was. *Ach*, this was a nightmare. "What should I do?"

Silas squeezed his shoulder. "You're a smart man. I'm sure you'll figure it out."

Bailey and her mother walked into the kitchen.

"What are you two discussing?" Bailey looked back and forth between Timothy and her step*dat*.

"Nothing anymore. Just man stuff. We're done now," Silas said.

"I should probably go soon." Timothy hadn't meant for his words to escape barely above a whisper.

He immediately noticed the disappointment in her eyes, and he hated it. Yet, at the same time, it sparked hope in his heart. She *wanted* him to be there just as much as he wanted to stay.

FOURTEEN

Bailey's folks returned to the living room, leaving just the two of them.

"They're probably encouraging the *kinner* to put their things away and get ready for bed," Bailey said.

Aaron, Bailey's younger half-brother, approached them. Timothy guessed he was around five years old. The boy held his hand out, palm up, and a dead fly was in the center. His bottom lip protruded.

"Whatcha got there?" Timothy asked, crouching down in front of the boy.

"It's Barney, my pet fly." The boy sniffled. "*Dat* killed 'em."

Bailey gasped. "*Dat* killed your pet fly?"

"He didn't know it was Barney." Aaron

affectionately touched the fly's unmoving wing.

"Barney?" Timothy stared at the dead insect. He shrugged. "I guess he kind of looks like a Barney."

"I named him that 'cuz *Dat* said he probably came from the barn."

"I see." Timothy nodded. "I have an idea."

"What is it?" Aaron wiped his nose on his shirtsleeve, nearly losing his fly in the process.

Timothy glanced at Bailey. "Why don't we give Barney a proper burial?"

"What's that?" Aaron's face scrunched up.

"When somebody we love dies, we have a funeral for them. Did you love Barney?"

The boy nodded solemnly.

"That settles it, then." He turned to Bailey. "Do you think we can find a small flat stick or maybe plastic? Something we can write on."

"I know just the thing." Bailey shot up and quickly ascended the stairs. A moment later she returned with something in her hand.

"I'm not even going to ask why there are tongue depressors in this house." He grinned.

She pushed his shoulder. "They're for craft projects, silly. Don't worry. Nobody's secretly studying to become a medical doctor."

Her comment elicited a giggle from Aaron, but he quickly became solemn again when he looked at his dead fly.

Timothy studied the boy. "Do you know when his birthday is?"

Aaron shook his head.

"How long have you had him?"

"He flew into my room two days ago. He came and said hello to me, but he stayed in the window, mostly. I think he was shy."

"Shy Barney." Timothy nodded. He pulled out a pen from his pocket. "Do you spell his name B-A-R-N-E-Y?"

Aaron shrugged. "I guess so."

Timothy finished writing on the wooden stick, then showed it to Aaron.

"I don't know what it says." The boy frowned.

"Right."

Bailey volunteered. "It says Barney Miller." She stopped. "Why does that name sound familiar?"

Timothy shrugged.

"Anyhow," she continued, "it says 'Barney Miller, two days old' and it has today's date."

"What's it for?"

Timothy ruffled the boy's hair. "That's his grave marker, buddy."

"His grave marker?" The boy's nose wrinkled.

Timothy nodded. "Let's go bury him."

Aaron's eyes expanded. "Right now?"

"If your sister will grab a flashlight." He looked at Bailey. "And a plastic spoon if you have one."

Her brow lowered in question.

"We'll use it as a shovel to dig his grave." Timothy glanced up at Bailey, noticing she suppressed a smile. He attempted to remain solemn for the boy's sake. Funerals were important business.

While Bailey left to fetch the necessary tools, he looked around. "Just a sec." He walked to the fireplace and shook the small matchbox. Good, it was almost empty. He opened the little box and set the three remaining matches on the mantel where the box had been.

Bailey handed him the items he'd asked for.

"Okay, just one more thing. Do you have a small scrap of fabric?" He held up the matchbox. "About this size?"

"Be right back." She ran up the stairs again, then return less than a minute later with a pretty blue material that matched some of the clothing her family wore.

"Perfect." He took the fabric and placed it in the matchbox. "Okay, Aaron, place Barney on top of the cloth inside the box."

The boy did as told.

Timothy closed the box with the dead fly inside. "I need you to carry the matchbox, er uh, Barney's casket to the burial site. Very carefully. Can you do that?"

Aaron nodded.

"*Kumm*, now." Timothy led the way to the door. "I'll hold the casket while you put your coat and gloves on."

Bailey helped the boy with his outerwear. She and Timothy donned their own, then they continued their solemn trek outside.

"Where should we bury him?" Timothy shined the flashlight, surveying the darkened landscape. "How about by your *mamm's* flowers? Do you think he would like that?" He glanced at the boy, who held his oldest sister's hand.

"*Jah.*" He nodded.

Their breath crystalized and swirled upward as the chill of winter descended.

Timothy, Bailey, and Aaron all crouched down near Kayla's rose bushes. He asked Bailey for the spoon, then handed it to Aaron. "Okay. You'll have to dig the grave. Do you think you can do that?"

The boy nodded, setting the box down on the dirt that had now gathered faint ice crystals.

"About this deep." He indicated about four inches.

When Aaron completed his task, Timothy instructed him to lower the casket into the small hole. Timothy held the grave marker in place while he instructed Aaron to fill the hole back up.

"I think we should say a prayer." Timothy glanced to Bailey, who nodded, still suppressing a smile.

He held out his hands for each of them to take, then they all bowed their heads. "*Her Gott, denki* for blessing Aaron's life with little Barney. Help Aaron not to be sad. And may Barney rest in peace. Amen."

Both Bailey and Aaron added their amens. Aaron dropped his hand, but Timothy's and Bailey's hands remained connected.

"Could we sing a song?" Aaron looked at Bailey and Timothy.

"Sure." Timothy smiled. "What would you like to sing?"

"'*Gott ist die Liebe*.'"

"That would be perfect." Timothy began singing the song he'd known for as long as he could remember. Bailey and Aaron immediately joined in.

When they finished the song, he smiled at Bailey. He'd never forget the look of admiration in her eyes. Or the way her hand had lingered in his longer than necessary. It wasn't a pledge of undying love, but it was a start. And in spite of Silas's warnings, Timothy was determined to win back both Bailey's love *and* Silas's approval. With *Gott's* help, he was sure and certain he could do both.

With Barney's funeral complete, they entered the warm house once again.

And that was when Bailey knew she couldn't agree to marry Mark. Timothy was the one. Would Mark have a funeral for her little brother's pet fly? *Nee*, she didn't think so.

Jah, it was kind of silly. But it hadn't been silly for Aaron. Most of all, it showed Timothy's achingly beautiful heart. He genuinely cared.

Ach, how she loved this man! She could no longer deny it.

Which meant she needed to end things with Mark as soon as possible.

FIFTEEN

*B*ailey hadn't intended to stay that long at her *mamm's*. She'd woken up late, then *Aenti* Jenny needed her to work a while because one of her *kinner* had gotten sick and needed her at home. Now, it was afternoon, and home was still quite a ways off.

Every time an *Englisch* vehicle passed her, she shuttered. Could they even see in front of them in this crazy weather?

Bailey hadn't been anticipating a snow storm to blow in. When the white stuff had first begun coming down, she had considered turning the rig around. But she'd already stayed a day longer at *Mamm* and Silas's than she'd planned to, and she needed to get home. Tomorrow was an off-church Sunday, but Mark had said he would be coming by. It would be the perfect time to talk to him about the things that had been on her mind lately. Who knew, maybe he would change her mind.

Not likely, her heart echoed back. Timothy was right. Something wasn't working in her and Mark's relationship. She'd known it for a while, but could never pinpoint what exactly it was. But now she knew the truth of the matter. She was still in love with Timothy. And Mark, well, Mark was in love with his work. Or with making money, at any rate.

But she couldn't think about any of that right now. This treacherous journey demanded every ounce of her concentration.

"*Ach*! I can hardly see." She squinted through the windshield, thankful for the little wiper that threw the snow off.

Hopefully, drivers of *Englisch* vehicles could still see her flashing lights. Not only was the snow falling hard, but it had been accumulating along the road. If someone were to come up behind her too fast, they probably wouldn't be able to stop before plowing into her.

It seemed quieter in the buggy for some reason. Why? She briefly looked around, and then shivered when a blast of cold air seeped through the buggy's flap. And then she realized what was different. Her heater had stopped working. Which meant it was likely out of propane.

"Now's not the time." It wasn't as if complaining to a heater was going to help.

She felt the buggy dip, then jostle. Something wasn't right. She maneuvered the horse off the road and onto the side as quickly as she could, where it was hopefully safe. She hopped down from the buggy, fighting the chilly wind, and noticed the problem right away. Her wheel had been damaged by the pothole.

What would she do now?

She secured Peanut Butter to a metal mile marker that barely stuck up from the snowy ground, then scurried back into the buggy, shivering all the while. She checked under the seat. Hopefully, there would be an extra bottle of propane for the heater. *Please, Gott.* She sighed in relief when she found one. She quickly exchanged the propane. She pulled out the small lap quilt as well. At least she could keep reasonably warm if she stayed in the buggy.

Through her windshield, she saw an *Englisch* vehicle pull off the road a little ways beyond the horse. It was a *gut* thing Peanut Butter didn't spook easily.

A middle-aged *Englisch* man hurried to the buggy flap and attempted to knock on it. "Someone in there?"

"*Jah.*" She opened the flap.

"Would you like a ride somewhere?"

Fear gripped her. She'd heard and read stories about *maed* that had gone missing after accepting rides with strangers. *Mamm* had warned her many times *never* to accept rides with strangers. "No, thank you," she managed.

"Would my cell phone be of any use to you, then?" He pulled the device from his jacket pocket.

She received it gratefully. "*Ach, jah.*" Who

would she be able to get ahold of right now? The only one she could think of with a cell phone was Mark. She quickly dialed his number from memory.

He answered after several rings. "Mark Petersheim."

"Hello, Mark. This is Bailey. My buggy wheel broke and I'm on the side of the road. Can you come get me?"

"Where are you?"

"Just past the halfway mark coming from *mei mamm's*."

"*Ach*, Bailey, that's a long way. And I'm busy working right now. I can't just leave this order and take off. Could you call someone else?"

Unbelievable. "*Ach, jah.* I'll try." If only Timothy had a cell phone. He'd drop anything—*anything*—and come rescue her.

"Stay safe." The call ended.

Bailey stared at the phone.

"Got a ride?" The man rubbed his hands together. Bailey doubted his thin coat was doing him any *gut*.

"May I make just one more call?"

"Sure. But my battery on that thing is almost dead, so you might want to make it quick."

She hastily dialed the phone shanty closest to *Dat* and Nora's and left a message. She handed the phone back to the man. "Thank you."

"You sure I can't give you a ride?"

"*Jah*. Someone will come. Thanks." She watched as the man jogged back to his vehicle. He must be halfway to snowman status by now.

Bailey shivered. It was then she noticed that her dress had become damp, likely from when she stepped outside to examine the buggy wheel. And, of course, in her haste and being the scatterbrain that she sometimes was, she'd forgotten her wool shawl on the hook in the store. Now, all she had to protect her from the elements was her green dress and the small lap quilt she kept inside the buggy.

She should probably turn off the heater to conserve the propane, but it was too cold. If it could just last long enough for this snow to let up, then... *Then what, Bailey?* She still had the problem of her broken buggy wheel.

There was no guarantee that *Dat* would even check the phone shanty tonight, either. Which meant she could be stranded for quite a while.

If only Peanut Butter were a riding horse, too. Then she could hop on his back and ride home once the storm quelled. But the horse barely tolerated his harness and reins. He hated having anything on his back and refused a saddle or a rider. As a matter of fact, he'd thrown *Dat* twice. After that, he decided it wasn't worth risking life and limb. At least he'd been able to train him to pull a buggy.

Bailey closed her eyes and began to pray fervently. *Gott* knew her situation, but it wouldn't hurt to beseech Him right now.

Timothy should have declined the delivery today. And he *would* have, if the family hadn't needed his herbs. Why on earth hadn't he hired a driver? But he already knew why. He'd wanted to be alone with his thoughts.

155

Thoughts of his *grossmammi* and the possibility of her not being in their lives much longer. Thoughts of his conversation with Silas and the possibility of him stepping in and preventing a relationship between his step*dochder* and Timothy. Thoughts of beautiful Bailey and the possibility of her choosing to marry a man she didn't love.

He wiped the windshield with his gloved hand, attempting to eliminate the moisture his breath created on the window. Seeing outside was bad enough without his breath adding decreased visibility. He squinted.

Ach, were those flashing lights on the side of the road? He was about to pass the snow-capped vehicle, parked on the opposite side of the road, when he realized it was a buggy. It looked like someone was stranded.

Who would be out in this weather? Then he laughed at himself when he realized that *he* was out in this weather.

He lifted the flap on his buggy "truck" to hear if there was any traffic approaching. All seemed quiet. He maneuvered his "truck" to the other side of the road and parked behind the stranded vehicle. Like his own vehicle, the windows were fogged up. He noticed the vehicle was slightly tilted. Was that because it was on an incline or was something wrong with it?

As he approached the horse, its peanut-butter color came into view. *Ach*, it was Bailey's horse! He turned back and jogged to the vehicle, then whisked the flap open in a flash.

"Bailey!"

A startled gasp escaped her lips. Tears immediately surfaced in her eyes. "Timothy! *Ach*, you don't know how glad I am to see you! I thought I might be stranded out here all night."

"How long have you been on the side of the road?"

"I don't know. A couple of hours maybe?"

"And no one has stopped to help?"

"*Jah*, a few *Englischers*. I used a man's cell phone and called Mark."

Timothy looked around. "Where is he?"

"He said he had to work. So then I called and

left a message at *Dat's* phone shanty."

Timothy held back his uncharitable retort. He could wring this Mark guy's neck right about now.

"My wheel is broken, and Peanut Butter won't be ridden, or else I would have just left the buggy and gone home. But my shoes aren't *gut* for the snow, and *dumm* me left my wool shawl at the store. Thankfully, I had the lap quilt."

That was when he noticed she was shivering. "Doesn't your heater work?" He reached for her hand and realized that it was clammy. He needed to get her out of this weather as soon as possible.

"It must've gone out. I think I fell asleep."

He examined her. "Your dress is wet. *Kumm*, we need to get you out of this weather. I'll take you to your *dat's* since it's the closest for you. I brought the truck, so I have rope that I can attach the horse to. He can trot along behind us."

When she stepped down from the buggy, he yanked off his coat and settled it around her shoulders.

"But you'll need it," she protested.

"Wear it until you get to my buggy, then you can wrap yourself in the blanket I have. It would be best if you took off that wet dress."

She gasped.

"For goodness' sake, Bailey. I wouldn't stand here and watch or anything. And no one can see through that window. You can wrap yourself in the blanket. You'll be much warmer than with that wet thing on. Go ahead and get out of it, while I tie the horse on. And if your shoes and socks are wet, take those off too."

He lifted her into his buggy, thankful for the blast of warm air from his heater. She removed his coat and handed it back to him.

"The blanket's warm. Wrap it around you. I'll knock before I come back in. Change now."

He didn't *ask*. He wouldn't give her the opportunity to say no. Getting out of her wet clothes was imperative. Her lips had already begun to turn blue.

He sent up a silent prayer. "Please let Bailey be okay, *Gott*. And help her not to be bullheaded about changing out of her clothes. Because both

You and I know that if I have to do it for her, it would not be a *gut* thing."

He tied up the horse as quickly as possible, then hurried back to the buggy. He knocked. "Are you decent in there?"

"*Jah.*"

He hopped back in, securing the flap so no unnecessary frigid air would enter. He turned to Bailey. "Are you okay? How are you feeling?"

"Warmer."

"*Gut.*" He reached over and rubbed her blanket-clad arms and her back to try to create a little friction. "Does that help?"

She swallowed. "*Jah. Denki.*" Her lips trembled, as though she were about to burst into tears.

He jostled the reins and moved the rig back onto the road. "Your *dat* can come back and get the buggy when the weather is better. Let's get you home now."

SIXTEEN

Bailey didn't know how many times she'd thanked *Gott* since Timothy had shown up and rescued her on the side of the road, but it was probably close to a couple dozen, at least. She had trouble holding back her tears. What were the chances of her and Timothy being out on the same road at the same time in the same storm? It could only have been a *Gott* thing.

She was anxious to get home, but now that she was with Timothy, it really didn't matter where they were. How could she have doubted this *wunderbaar* man's love for her?

She'd snuggled closer to him when he'd draped his arm around her, once they'd turned off the main highway onto a less traveled road. She always loved back roads, especially this time of year when the barns and houses and trees all looked like they'd been bathed in marshmallow crème. Which made her hungry all of a sudden for rice crispy treats.

Timothy had always loved rice crispy treats. Ha! A dessert she could make on the stove that wouldn't require the use of Nora's oven. And if Nora hadn't used the ingredients in Bailey's absence this week, they would still be available. She smiled at the thought of making something yummy for Timothy. He certainly deserved to be spoiled after his gallantry.

Before she knew it, Timothy was pulling into the driveway. *Ach*, she'd never been so happy to be home. Especially with Timothy by her side.

She glanced down at her blanket-clad body. How on earth was she going to explain this to *Dat*? Particularly since he didn't know Timothy from Charlie Brown. The only thing he'd heard about Timothy in the past was how he'd broken Bailey's heart.

Jah, things could get sticky. Even without the

rice crispy treats.

Timothy brought the buggy to a halt right outside the front door. He jumped down and jogged around to her side. He opened the flap on the passenger side. "Cover up well."

She did as told, then before she knew it, he'd whisked her into his arms and carried her to the entrance. He pounded on the front door. No two knocks this time.

Dat opened the door and groaned the moment he saw her. She must look a sight.

"I found her broken down on the side of the road. She needs fresh dry clothes and a warm fire." He deposited Bailey just inside the door. "I'm going to get the horses out of this weather. They could probably use rest and a treat."

"There's a bucket of oats near the first stall," *Dat* said, gratefulness shining in his eyes.

And just like that, Timothy disappeared, closing the door behind him. No doubt he was anxious to warm himself by the fire as well.

Her *vatter* examined her. "I'm guessing you have quite a story to tell."

She nodded. "*Jah*. For sure."

"Why don't you go change into something dry first?"

"Okay." She wouldn't tell *Dat* that she wore nothing more than her undergarments beneath Timothy's fleece blanket. Just the thought of divulging that information nearly brought on a panic attack. Not that she'd ever had a panic attack or knew exactly what it was, even. But she could *imagine* having one while telling her *vatter* something so embarrassing.

Once she was cloistered in her room, she made the mistake of looking into her mirror. *Eek*! Oh my. To think she'd looked like this the entire time she'd been with Timothy was even more embarrassing than wearing nothing under the blanket. She'd better whip herself into shape and fast.

She removed her outer bonnet and her soggy flat prayer *kapp* first. Somehow, moisture must've gotten under her bonnet. No wonder she'd had such a difficult time staying warm. Then she found a dress in deep teal green, Timothy's favorite color, and threw it over her head, then quickly fastened on the matching cape and apron. She hastily brushed her hair into submission. Fortunately, she'd become an expert at twisting her hair into a bun and sticking the pins in to hold it tight. She grabbed one of her clean, freshly-starched *kapps* and fastened it in place.

She glanced in the mirror again. *Now*, she was ready to face Timothy—the man she loved. A smile curved on her lips.

When she heard Timothy enter the house, she made haste to meet him. He deserved a proper introduction. And a whole lot more. But he'd get that later.

The moment their eyes met and held, Bailey practically melted into a puddle of gooey chocolate right there on the hallway floor. How did Timothy have that effect on her?

Her *vatter* cleared his throat, breaking the love spell. *Hardly.*

"Bailey, why don't you invite your Good Samaritan to join us for supper?" *Dat* suggested. "I don't think Nora would mind another dinner guest." He arched his brow in his *fraa's* direction.

"No, of course not." Nora smiled, as she set plates around the table. "Especially since he rescued you in that awful weather."

"I..." What would Mark say if he showed up and saw her eating with another man? Of course, her family was present too, so maybe it wouldn't seem inappropriate. Oh, why was she even concerned about what Mark would think? *Because he still thinks you're going to marry him.* Right. There was that.

As they stepped further into the living room, she glanced at Timothy, whose expression seemed hopeful yet unassuming.

"*Jah*, okay." She nodded to her *vatter* and Nora.

Bailey turned to Timothy. "Would you like to join us for supper?"

"I would be honored." His intense gaze held sincerity.

More and more, she was reminded of all the things she'd loved about Timothy. She'd agree to marry him today if he asked.

"I should introduce you," Bailey said to Timothy, as he divested himself of his outerwear and entered the living room.

"*Dat*, Nora, this is Timothy Stoltzfoos. He's...uh...he's..."

"I'm from Bishop Bontrager's *g'may*," Timothy volunteered. "Nice to meet you."

Dat's grin widened. "Timothy." He nodded. "I believe we already know each other. You run the Stoltzfoos Greenhouse, right?"

"That's right." Timothy pumped *Dat's* outstretched hand. "I ordered non-GMO seed for you earlier this year." He shook his head. "I had no idea you were Bailey's *vatter*."

"That would be me."

Timothy grinned. "Come to think of it, there was something about you that looked familiar to me, but I couldn't quite put my finger on it. Now I know. I saw Bailey in you."

"She's a pretty girl, *ain't so*?" *Dat* winked at her.

"*Dat*!" Bailey protested, certain her cheeks were all kinds of crimson. "You shouldn't—"

"I've always thought so," Timothy agreed.

"Timothy..." But this time her voice emerged as a whisper.

"If you two are finished embarrassing poor Bailey, supper's ready." Nora slung a comforting arm around Bailey's shoulders. "You just never know what's going to come out of their mouths, do you?"

Bailey huffed. "*Nee.*"

"Timothy, I really think you should stay here for the night. That storm is pretty bad and I know that Bailey would never forgive herself if something happened to you on her account," Bailey's *vatter* remarked.

"He's right, you know." Bailey smiled.

"I hate to go back out in that again." Timothy grimaced, stretching his hands to warm them by the fireplace. "I might just take you up on that offer. Is there a phone shanty nearby?"

"Up the road about half a mile, on the left. You're welcome to ride Picasso bareback," Josiah offered.

"Picasso?"

"The painted horse." He laughed. "You'll understand when you see her."

"Alrighty then." He moved to the door and donned his coat and hat. "I guess I'll be back in a bit." He winked at Bailey before heading out the door.

Timothy maneuvered the horse onward, keeping to the left side of the lane, his eyes peeled. A half mile wasn't *this* far, was it? Had he missed the phone shanty somewhere along the way? *Nee*, he didn't think so. He shined his flashlight into the surrounding woods.

Ach, it was tough to determine anything in near-zero visibility. Especially on land he was unfamiliar with. Should he continue on or turn around and head back? *Nee*, he shouldn't head back. He needed to let *Mamm* and *Dat* know where he was, so they wouldn't worry.

He finally spotted a tall snow-covered lump. It could only be the phone shanty. He sighed in relief. "We found it, boy. You'll stay there while I make my call, right?" he said, petting the gentle horse.

He found the door handle and slipped inside, then quickly dialed the number of their family phone. Unlike this shanty, their phone was just at the end of the driveway. A buggy drove past as he was notifying his folks of his plan. Were the Beachys expecting company tonight? After leaving his message, he felt much better about staying the night. He wouldn't be able to rest well if he knew his parents would be worrying about him.

He peeked out the shanty's small window. The buggy was long gone. But where was Picasso? He opened the door and began to step out. A strong gust of wind yanked the door out of his hand, then immediately snapped back and struck him on the forehead. The force caused him to stumble backward into the shanty, hitting the back of his head on the table. He felt his body falling to the ground as if in slow motion.

SEVENTEEN

"So Timothy is...?" *Dat* eyed Bailey curiously from the hickory rocker.

Bailey glanced at Nora, who read a book on the couch. Her two oldest girls washed dishes at the kitchen sink, and the youngest two played in their room.

"He's my old beau." She bit her bottom lip.

"The one who broke your heart?" *Dat's* eyebrow shot up.

"That would be the one."

"Something isn't connecting here."

"*Jah*, I know." She sighed, then stared at her *vatter*. "I'm still in love with him, *Dat*."

"I see." *Dat* nodded. "Well, I guess that complicates things a little, doesn't it?"

"For sure." She released a breath. "I'm breaking up with Mark next time I see him."

"You're certain about this?"

"More than anything."

"Okay, then." He shrugged. "You're an adult and capable of making your own decisions. Do you know what you're going to say to Mark? Have you prayed about this?"

"*Dat*, I've been praying since the day I ran into Timothy. I was angry with him at first, but now I've gotten over it. He apologized for what happened back then, and I've forgiven him. He's a *wunderbaar* man and he truly loves me. He's caring. He's *gut* with *kinner*. He even had a fly funeral."

"A *what*?"

"*Ach*, I'll tell you about it later." She laughed.

"I can tell you're happier than usual."

"You couldn't even believe how happy I am."

A knock on the door stole their attention. *Dat* smiled. "It looks like your guy's back." He shot up from his rocker to open the door.

"Already?" Bailey frowned.

Dat pulled on the door. "Mark. You here to see Bailey?"

"Uh, yeah." He stepped inside and *Dat* shut the door.

It seemed this night could get even more interesting.

"*Kumm* in," *Dat* said.

"Okay. I can't stay long. I just wanted to make sure Bailey found her way back home."

"Yep. Here I am. At home and in one piece." *No thanks to you.* Did she sound as sassy as she felt?

"*Gut.*" He nodded. Apparently, her sarcasm had been lost on Mark. "Well, okay then. I plan to stop by tomorrow, Bailey, if that's okay. In the afternoon?"

"Sure. That's fine." She wasn't quite ready for *that* conversation yet, anyhow. Especially with Timothy present.

"See ya, then." He stepped back out and *Dat* shut the door behind him.

Dat turned to her, looking amused. "Well, that was short and sweet."

Now, if Timothy would just return.

Bailey went to the window and stared out. The snow falling made it near impossible to see anything. And then...was that a buggy heading toward the house? She squinted.

"*Dat, kumm* here."

He moved to the window and looked out. "Looks like Mark's back. Wait. Is that Picasso with him?"

Bailey and her *vatter* both rushed to the door. *Dat* flung it open and they stepped outside.

"Found your horse wondering around out yonder. I threw a rope on him and brought him back," Mark called out.

"Where's Timothy?" Bailey looked to her *vatter*.

Dat hollered to Mark. "There wasn't someone with the horse?"

"No. I didn't see anyone."

"Where did you find him?"

"About halfway between here and the phone shanty."

Dat turned to her. "I want you to stay here, Bailey. I'm going to go investigate."

They both moved back into the house. *Dat* quickly donned his heavy coat, gloves, scarf, and boots, topping the ensemble off with a black beanie, then his wool hat.

"Nora, I'm going out to see if everything's all right with Timothy. Mark's out there, so I'll have him come with me. Make sure this one stays inside." He nodded toward Bailey.

"*Dat.*"

"No arguing. You've been out in that too long today already. I'm not going to let anything happen to you. Do you understand?"

Bailey wanted to protest. Timothy rescued *her* on the road. How could she just sit idly by? Especially when *Dat* was worried. *Why* was *Dat* worried? Just because Picasso had gotten away didn't mean Timothy was in danger, did it?

"You'll do more good if you pray," *Dat* advised.

Pray. "*Jah.* Okay."

"I'm sure Timothy is fine, but he may need

help finding his way back. He's not familiar with this area. That's all. So don't fret." *Dat* finally stepped out the door.

Bailey watched through the window until *Dat* and his flashlight disappeared into the blinding snow. *Gott, please be with Dat and Timothy and Mark. Watch over them.*

EIGHTEEN

Bailey hadn't left the window since *Dat* had disappeared from sight twenty minutes ago. *Everything's fine.* She told herself. *Picasso just got away from Timothy. No big deal.*

If only she could believe her affirmations.

Finally, Mark's buggy surfaced through the snow once again. They were back! But did they have Timothy with them?

Mark stopped in front of the house, and tied his horse to the hitching post out front.

Bailey hurried to open the door. She watched as *Dat* slipped his arm around Timothy's back. Mark did the same on Timothy's other side. They slowly walked to the house.

Bailey moved out of the way, puzzled as to

what may have transpired. Her heart sped up. What was wrong with Timothy?

"What happened, *Dat*? Is Timothy okay?"

They took him to the couch, then helped him sit down. Timothy seemed to just stare blankly.

"*Dat*?" Why was no one talking to her? She needed answers. Now!

Dat approached her. "We found him in the phone shanty. It appears he was knocked out. He has a cut on his forehead. I'm not sure what happened."

"Did you ask him?" Why wasn't Timothy speaking? What on earth was going on?

She marched over to where Timothy sat. Mark sat next to him, looking back and forth from Bailey to Timothy. Seemed like she wasn't the only one who was puzzled.

"Timothy? What happened? Are you okay?"

Mark frowned. "He hasn't said anything." He stared at Bailey. "Who is he?"

"Timothy Stoltzfoos."

"And...? How do *you* know him?"

She didn't want to have this conversation with

Mark right now. She wanted time alone with Timothy. She reached out and touched his face. "Timothy? It's Bailey."

He didn't respond. Tears pricked her eyes. "*Dat*! What's wrong with him?"

Dat came near. "Shh...calm down, Bailey. He'll be okay. I think he just has a concussion."

"Why isn't he talking? Does he need to go to the hospital?"

"Not in this weather. I think he'll be fine." Her father shook his head. "His brain is just *ferhoodled* at the moment."

She grasped one of Timothy's hands and held it between her own. "But he's going to be okay, right?"

"I believe he will with time. Concussions don't usually last long. He's likely in a fog right now or his mind may be trying to piece together what happened."

"Timothy." Why wouldn't he look at her? *Ach*, she wanted to break down in tears. She wanted to pull Timothy close. She wanted to tell him everything was going to be okay. But she couldn't do *any* of that with Mark sitting next to them.

"Bailey, why don't you and Mark go talk in the kitchen? I'll sit here with Timothy until you're done."

She glanced at Timothy, then at Mark. "*Jah*. Okay."

She reluctantly released Timothy's hand, then she and Mark walked to the kitchen.

Mark took a seat at the table, staring up at her. "Are you ready to talk to me now?"

She frowned, then sat across from him at the table. "*Jah*." She squeezed her eyes shut. "Timothy is an old friend, *nee*, old beau, who lives in *mei mamm's* district."

Mark's lips pulled downward. "And he's *here* because...? Help me out here, Bailey. What's going on?"

She huffed. "He rescued me on the side of the road. He saved me when I was about to freeze to death."

"Don't be overdramatic, Bailey."

"I'm not." She ground the words out. "My

buggy wheel broke. If Timothy hadn't come along, who knows how long I would have been stuck out there in the cold? My heater had stopped working. I was wet. It wasn't a *gut* situation. I just thank *Gott* that Timothy happened upon me when he did."

"So, that's it?" Mark stared at her. His lack of concern for her wellbeing astounded her. "I have a feeling there's more to the story that you're not telling me."

So much more, in fact. She might as well come out with it. "Mark." She frowned. "I...I'm sorry."

"Sorry for what?"

"I can't marry you. Not now."

"Not now?"

"*Nee*. Not ever."

"What...so...you're breaking up with me?" His frowned deepened. He clearly hadn't been expecting this.

She hadn't been expecting this.

She forged on. "I can't continue in this relationship with you. I realized that I'm still in love with Timothy."

181

"You're still..." He worked his jaw. "Really, Bailey? You're really dumping me. After all this time?"

"I'm sorry. Continuing this relationship would be unfair to you. I'm in love with Timothy. And I don't think that you really love me, either."

"I can't believe you're doing this." Mark swallowed, clenching his fists. He stood and stepped away from the table. "I guess there's no reason for me to be here, then. Goodbye, Bailey."

Her gaze followed as Mark slunk out the door, not even bothering to say goodbye to her *vatter*. Not that she could blame him. He had just been dealt a tough blow. She reckoned that she wouldn't be up for talking to anyone either, had she been in his shoes.

A part of her was sad. She wished Mark well. Really, she did. Hopefully, *Der Herr* would send along the perfect person just for him. All she knew was that it wasn't her. *Nee*. The perfect person for her—the *only* person for her—was Timothy.

Poor Timothy.

She hurried back to the couch. "Any change?" she asked her *vatter*.

"*Jah*. Actually. He said a couple of words."

Excitement bubbled in her chest. "He did?"

"Yes. I think it's just a matter of time."

"What did he say?"

Dat shrugged. "The horse."

"The horse? Picasso? Was he trying to tell you what happened, maybe?"

"I don't know. Maybe. I told him that the horse was safe in the barn now. I think he might have been worried about it."

"Do you think he understands what we're saying?"

"I'm not sure, Bailey."

"*Dat*, I don't want to leave him to sleep out here by himself. Is it okay if I stay here with him?"

"He'll probably be okay, Bailey."

"But what if he tries to leave or something? He's not in his right mind." She frowned. "I wish he would wake up from this."

She snapped her fingers in front of his face. "Timothy."

"Bailey, don't do that," *Dat* warned.

Timothy turned his head toward her. "Bailey?"

The word came out sluggish, but he'd said her name.

"*Dat*!"

"I know. I heard." Dat nodded.

She took Timothy's hand in hers, stroking it lightly. "Timothy, do you know me?"

A confused look flashed across his face, then a slight smile turned up at the side of his lips. "I think so."

Gut, he was showing emotion now.

She caressed his cheek and stared into his eyes. "I love you."

"I hope so." A tiny smile accompanied Timothy's words.

Bailey laughed. "*Dat*, I think he's coming back."

"It appears so." *Dat* smiled.

"Timothy, do you remember the shoeboxes?"

Timothy's brow furrowed. Was he trying to concentrate? "Shoeboxes?"

"*Jah*. The charity project for the poor *kinner* in other countries?"

"I can't...I don't know." Timothy frowned.

184

"Bailey, it's probably best not to overwhelm him with too much information," *Dat* advised. "It'll come back to him in time. Let him find his bearings." He looked at Timothy. "It's okay. You don't have to figure out everything right now, Timothy."

Dat stood. "I'm going to leave you two. Nora put the others down a while ago. Bailey, if you'd rather sleep here on the couch and make up your bed for Timothy, that would be okay. It might be better if he has privacy, especially in the morning when everyone is up and around."

"*Jah*, okay. I think that's a *gut* idea. *Guten nacht, Dat*." She watched her *vatter* walk toward his bedroom. "Wait, *Dat*. Do you think Timothy will need help getting to the bedroom?"

"If he does, come knock on my door and I'll help."

"*Jah*, okay."

The door to *Dat's* bedroom clicked closed.

Her fingers lightly trailed Timothy's forearm. "Are you tired?"

"*Jah*. A little." He rubbed his head.

"Do you want to go to sleep already?"

His lips turned down. "Not yet."

"Okay. What do you want to do?"

"Don't know."

"Do you know what happened? How you got hurt?" Her fingers feathered across his injured brow. *Ach*, how she wished she could make everything better for him! Seeing him in this state caused her heart to squeeze tightly inside her chest. She didn't like that feeling at all.

"*Nee*."

"I'm going to get a drink of water. Would you like some?" She stood from the couch. She had to do something with herself.

"I'll come too." He stood slowly, his hand holding his forehead. He winced.

"Do you have a headache?"

"*Jah*." He squeezed his eyes closed.

She hated seeing her beloved in pain. "You don't have to come with me. You can stay here."

"I want to." He reached for her hand.

She brought his hand to her lips, then stared into his eyes. "You're going to be okay, Timothy."

She wasn't sure whether she was speaking more for *his* benefit or for her own. Because, if he didn't make a full recovery...

Ach, she wouldn't think of that now. He *would* recover. He had to.

Bailey closed her eyes. *Gott, please help Timothy to recover quickly and let him be able to return to normal.* But she knew in her heart that even if Timothy never fully recovered, she'd still love him with all her heart.

NINETEEN

*B*ailey wasn't sure and certain how many times she'd prayed over the last few days, but it had been many. And looking at Timothy now, she believed *Der Herr* heard and answered every single prayer.

It was funny how one serious incident could rearrange your entire schedule.

Dat, along with an *Englisch* driver who owned a trailer, had gone to retrieve Bailey's buggy the day after Timothy's accident. While *Dat* was out and about, he'd informed *Mamm* and Silas about the entire ordeal, and they'd promised to pass the information on to Timothy's family. He'd also let them know that Bailey wouldn't be helping out at the store that week. She hated leaving her aunt in the lurch during one of the busiest weeks of the year, but it couldn't be helped. Thankfully, *Aenti* Jenny managed to get Emily to fill in for Bailey.

Dat, Silas, *Onkel* Paul, and their friend Michael Eicher finally took their turkey hunting trip. Timothy was disappointed, because he'd wanted to go along to snag a turkey for his *mamm*. *Dat* shot an extra bird and delivered it to Timothy's family on his behalf. Each family would have a fresh turkey for Thanksgiving this year.

Timothy and Bailey stayed at *Dat* and Nora's for a full three days, because *Dat* wanted Timothy to fully recover from his head trauma. *Dat* had borrowed the *Englisch* driver's cell phone to research concussions and learned that it was important not to overdo it physically or mentally after an injury like Timothy's. Timothy chose not to see a doctor, and *Dat* honored his wishes.

Timothy hadn't seemed to mind spending extra time with her and getting to know her father's side of the family and vice versa. But now that the due date was nearing for the shoebox project, he was beginning to worry that they wouldn't be able to complete their boxes in time.

Bailey determined to go with Timothy to his *grossmammi's* today. She and his *mammi* planned to go shopping to purchase the items for the shoeboxes. Timothy had wanted to go along, and as much as Bailey desired that too, she'd discouraged it. Instead, she'd put him in charge of wrapping the empty shoeboxes while they were out and about gathering the items to fill them with.

Bailey now wondered how many he'd wrapped as she pushed a cart down the aisle at the dollar store, keeping an eye out for the items on their list.

"Look at this, Bailey," Timothy's *grossmammi* held up a small stuffed animal. She pushed a little button and a child's voice recited a bedtime prayer. *Mammi* smiled. "Do you think this would be *gut* to put into the boxes?"

Bailey loved the enthusiasm on *Mammi's* face. "*Jah.* I like it. Let's get several."

Bailey found pens, crayons, a four pack of notebooks, and several other items. She checked each one off their list once she added them to the shopping cart.

"This is fun," *Mammi* smiled.

"It is, isn't it? I just wish Timothy could have come."

"There will be other times. Right now, though, we'll enjoy our girl time out."

"Yes, we will. And I think we should do this more often. What do you think?" She wanted to give *Mammi* something to look forward to.

"That sounds like a *gut* plan." *Mammi* patted Bailey's hand.

Ach, Timothy would be so happy to see the joy radiating from his *grossmammi's* face.

"We're almost done here. We can stop by Walmart for the clothes next," Bailey said.

"Okay."

Bailey frowned. "Timothy had wanted to take us out for a meal. What do you say if we pick up some Chinese food and take it home? Then we can still enjoy a fancy meal together."

"I love Chinese food. That sounds like a *gut* idea, my dear." She turned to stare at Bailey. "Now, tell me something. When are you and *mei gross sohn* going to get hitched?"

Bailey giggled. "Well, I reckon he'll have to ask me first."

"What is that *bu* waiting for? You two are both baptized already, *ain't so*?"

"*Jah*, we are."

"Well, then, it looks like a visit with the leaders might be in order. I'll have to suggest that to Timothy."

Bailey couldn't hide her smile. "If you want to do that, *Mammi,* I'm not going to stop you."

"And this is the last one." Timothy handed the final box filled with shoeboxes to the charity representative. Satisfaction filled his entire being.

Ach, it was *wunderbaar* to be back to his normal self. He felt so *gut* he wanted to do his double-dip flip off the swing like he'd done back when he was in school. He wouldn't, of course. Bailey kept a tight leash on him and had a fit anytime he spoke of doing anything remotely strenuous. It was probably for the best.

"I wonder when we'll hear back from the

kinner we sent letters to," Bailey mused aloud, after they'd watched the van pull away from the library.

"I'm not sure, but I'm guessing it'll probably take a couple of months. You'll have to be patient, *lieb.*" *Ach*, if only they were alone. He'd love to take her into his arms right now.

"My *dat* wanted me to be sure to invite you over for Christmas. Not that I wouldn't anyhow." She smiled. "We're going to have a large gathering."

"Has your step*dat* said anything lately?"

"About us?"

"*Jah.*"

"I think you've gotten back into Silas's *gut* graces after *Dat* told him how you rescued me when I was stranded in the snowstorm. And since I told him that I'd broken up with Mark and that I was in love with you." She shrugged. "What can he say?"

"Oh, he had plenty to say last time. I just don't want to disappoint him. Or you."

"Disappoint *me*? Timothy, you are the most

wunderbaar man I know. You have the most *wunderbaar* heart that I've seen. You are a giver. Not only do you give of your time and your talent, but you give your heart and soul. Look how you've brought joy back into your *grossmammi's* life. Into *my* life. Into the lives of all those *kinner* receiving the shoeboxes."

He reached for her hand. "Can we get married as soon as possible?"

"I'd like nothing better."

"*Gut*, because I've spoken with Bishop Bontrager and he's agreed to marry us in three weeks if everyone is in agreement."

"You're joking, right?"

"*Nee*, I'm not joking. I wouldn't kid about something as important as that."

"So, *before* Christmas?"

He grinned. "That's right."

"I get to spend Christmas as your *fraa*?" Her cheeks blossomed like the fuchsia roses he grew in his greenhouse.

He loved the way her eyes seemed to hold nothing but admiration for him. *Ach*, how he loved this woman with everything in him. "The best Christmas gift ever. After the gift of our Saviour, of course."

"What about your folks?"

He shrugged. "They're all for it. Since they realized you had no intentions of becoming *Englisch,* and saw how you cared for me after the accident, I don't think they have any *gut* reason not to love you."

"*Love* me?"

"*Jah,* they love you, Bailey."

She blew out a breath. "Where will we live?"

"*Mammi* has said she doesn't like living in the *dawdi haus* all alone. She offered to give it up for us until we find a place of our own. She's going to move into my room in the big house, which, I think will help her feel less lonely. I'm thinking we'll probably stay in the *dawdi haus* for a few months or for as long as it takes for us to find property to build a house on. I have enough money saved up for a decent down payment."

"Wow. We have a lot of work to do between now and then. Are you sure you're up to it? I don't want you to overdo it."

"We have a lot of helpers. Who will you ask to be your side sitters?"

"I'm thinking definitely Emily. And maybe Martha?"

He nodded. "Okay. I'll probably have my *brieder*."

"I only foresee one problem."

"What's that?"

"*Mamm* isn't going to be up for preparing the house for a wedding. I suppose we could possibly have it at *Dat* and Nora's."

"You better ask your *mamm* first. You know she'll think it's an honor to have your wedding there. My *mamm* will help, and probably *Mammi* too, if we let her. And I'm sure your aunts will be willing to help out. And you *know* Silas isn't going to let your *mamm* overdo it."

"*Ach*, you're right."

"We're being published at church this Sunday. Do you think you can keep it a secret until then?"

"What about my folks, and yours?"

"We'll tell them, of course. But first..." He

looked around, then shook his head. "*Kumm...*"

He urged her to follow him back into the library, and down the steps to the lower level where the boxes had been before they'd been given to the charity organization. The lower level was empty and quiet.

Bailey smiled at him. "What are we doing?"

"Something I've been wanting to do all day." Timothy pulled Bailey near, closed his eyes, and lowered his lips to hers. Her kiss was soft and tender and sweet. And something he'd never tire of all the days of his life.

TWENTY

Bailey hadn't been prepared for *Dat's* proclamation the moment she and Timothy walked through the door.

"Guess who's coming for Christmas!" The joy on her *vatter's* face gave away the answer.

"*Dawdi* Alvin and *Mammi* Ada!" She was certain her enthusiasm mirrored her *vatter's*. "Really?"

Timothy grinned, sharing in their excitement.

"That's right." *Dat* nodded.

The warmth inside *Dat's* house compelled her and Timothy to remove their coats and scarves. "They haven't been here since your wedding, right? So they've never seen the *bopplin*?"

"*Nee.*"

Jennifer Spredemann

"I remember when I met them for the first time. I loved them right away." *Ach*, she felt her smile couldn't get any wider.

"Me too," her *vatter* teased.

"*Dat*! You don't remember that."

"How do you know? I could."

She snorted.

"Is anyone coming with them? Any of my aunts and uncles?"

"I'm not sure. But your grandparents should be here for the big get-together, Lord willing."

"Oh, that'll be so much fun!"

"I know, right?"

Bailey always laughed when her *vatter* used terms carried over from his *Englischer* days. Of course, he'd spent nearly half of his life in that world. She understood how things from the past wouldn't just disappear once he joined the Amish again. Besides, he'd barely returned four years ago.

"Well, do you think they can be here a little early? Like the week before Christmas?" She turned and shared a smile with Timothy.

"Why?" *Dat* looked back and forth at each of

them. "Wait. You're not—"

Timothy stepped forward, his countenance radiating pure joy. "I asked Bailey to marry me and she said yes. Bishop Bontrager plans to have the deacon announce it to the *g'may* in our district this Sunday."

"Well, it looks like we'll be visiting this Sunday, then." *Dat* pulled her close and kissed the top of her head. "Congratulations, kiddo!"

"Thanks, *Dat*."

He looked to Timothy. "Wow. You don't waste any time, do you?"

"I first got the notion to marry Bailey when we were sixteen. I don't think I'm going to break any records for speed." Timothy chuckled.

"Did you already tell your *mamm* and Silas?"

"*Jah*. We told them first. They're happy for us."

"You're having the wedding at your *mamm's* then, right?"

"That's right."

"Make sure to let them know that Nora and I will help out any way we can."

"*Gut.* Because I'm sure they could use the extra help. Especially since *Mamm* had little Caleb not that long ago. She's pretty much back to normal now, but I know Silas is still overprotective of her."

"Well, then. It looks like I have a phone call to make. If your *Mammi* and *Dawdi* are going to come early, I'd better let them know as soon as possible. I don't think they'd miss their *grossdochder's* wedding for the world." He rubbed his hands together. "And won't Nora be surprised when she returns home from grocery shopping."

"I can't believe you're getting married before me. That's so not fair," Emily complained to Bailey, as she helped prepare the centerpieces for the wedding reception.

Bailey laughed. "Well, if you weren't so picky, you could've been married by now. You've ridden home with a dozen *buwe* from this district."

"And none of them is the right one. You're lucky. You sure found Timothy easily." She carefully arranged the rocks in the glass dish.

"I wouldn't say easily."

Emily fastened a hand on her hip. "He was the first *bu* you dated!"

"But not the only *bu*. Hey, maybe I should introduce you to Mark Petersheim."

"Really, Bailey? You'd want me to date your castoff?"

"Well, just because he wasn't right for me doesn't mean he won't be right for you."

"I thought you said he was already married to his work. And that he was a *dummkopp*."

"Right. Scratch that."

Emily came close and whispered, "Well, what about poor Martha? She'll likely never find a husband."

"Maybe a handsome widower will roll into town."

Emily laughed out loud. "You've been reading those books again, haven't you?"

"*Nee*. I haven't read any in quite a while, actually. No time."

"How many people do you think will be here?"

"I don't know. With my two families and Timothy's family—who knows who might show up from Pennsylvania? And then, of course, there is our *g'may* and *Dat's g'may. Ach*, it could be quite large."

"What are you and Timothy gonna do with all the presents? I doubt there will be room in that tiny *dawdi haus*."

"We can store them at *Mamm's* or *Dat's* until we need them. I don't think it's a big deal."

Martha joined them. "Are you two done yakking? I've done twice as many centerpieces as either of you has done."

"Don't be a pill, Martha," Emily said. "We won't get many more times together like this, especially as single women. Let us enjoy it."

Timothy walked into the shop with *Onkel* Jaden at his side. "It looks like you ladies are whipping this place into shape. It looks *gut*."

"Why, *denki*." Bailey curtseyed.

"Sorry, Emily, but I need to steal Bailey away for a moment. I need her opinion on something. But I'll leave Jaden here to assist you with anything you need."

"Have you two even met my *onkel* Jaden from Pennsylvania? He arrived with mei *grosseldre* yesterday."

"*Nee*, we haven't." Emily urged Martha forward.

"I think Jaden's around your age, Martha."

When *Aenti* Martha looked up, Bailey hadn't expected a small gasp to emerge from her lips. In turn, *Onkel* Jaden dipped his head.

"*Gut* to meet you, Martha." He managed.

Ach, if Bailey didn't know any better, she'd think the two of them were sweet on each other. She nodded to Emily. "And this is Emily."

"Nice to meet you too." He politely smiled at Emily, but his gaze trailed back to Martha.

"Bailey and I will be right back." Timothy grasped her hand and they stepped out of the shop that Silas and *Onkel* Paul used for their metalwork. It was the perfect size for a large reception.

Timothy turned to Bailey. "It looks like we should pair those two up for some of the games."

Bailey grinned. "You noticed too? I was thinking the same thing." She looked around and saw that he'd led her to the barn. "Hey, what are we doing in here?"

Timothy opened his buggy and gestured for her to enter. He slid in beside her, then closed the door.

"Where are we going?"

"Nowhere. I just had to steal away for a moment with my soon-to-be *fraa*. It's much quieter in here."

"*Jah*, it's peaceful."

"Are you ready for tomorrow, *lieb*?" His thumb lightly roamed over her hand,

"*Ach*, ready as I'll ever be." Tears pricked her eyes. "We've been anticipating this day for way too long. I thought it would never happen."

He brushed away her tears. "You and me both. But it's finally happening, Bailey. After tomorrow, our lives will never be the same again. We begin our own little family."

"It'll be the best day of my life."

"Mine too." Timothy pulled Bailey onto his

lap, threaded his fingers through the hair under her prayer *kapp*, and indulged in sweet kisses that held a promise of passion that could only be fulfilled after tomorrow.

When they would become man and wife.

EPILOGUE

Christmas day...

Becoming Mrs. Timothy Stoltzfoos had to be one of the best things Bailey had ever done. Of course, she supposed every bride of one week likely said the same thing. *Nee*, Timothy wasn't perfect. Neither was she, of course. But love was.

They hoped next year by this time, *Gott* willing, that they'd be holding a little one in their arms. But only *Der Herr* knew what the future held. Maybe He wouldn't bless them with *kinner* of their own making right away. Maybe He would have them visit one of the places their shoeboxes shipped to and they'd adopt one or several *kinner* from an orphanage. Something they'd already discussed.

All Bailey knew was that *Gott* had given them enough love to share with others, and that was what they wished to do, whichever way *Der Herr* led.

She'd been thrilled to introduce Timothy to her family from Pennsylvania, who coincidentally knew some of *his* family in Pennsylvania. A common occurrence in Amish culture. It seemed anytime there was a get-together of this kind, everyone attempted to figure out how and if they were related.

Just yesterday, Emily had informed her that her sister—Bailey's *aenti* Martha—and Bailey's *onkel* Jaden had agreed to exchange letters. Bailey hoped it would be the beginning of something *wunderbaar* for her *alt maedel aenti* and bachelor *onkel*. It seemed only right, since the both of them were school teachers and all. They seemed to have much in common.

As breakfast finished and the morning quieted down, all of the family, adults and children alike, had gathered around, and her *grossdawdi* read the Christmas story from the book of Luke. They each listened intently, reverently, as he read of Mary and Joseph's journey to Bethlehem, the shepherds being visited by angels, and the glorious, yet humble birth of the Saviour of the world.

Grossdawdi finished off their devotion by reading a few other passages on giving. First, from James. *Every good gift and every perfect gift is from above, and cometh down from the Father of lights, with whom is no variableness, neither shadow of turning.*

From Luke. *Give, and it shall be given unto you; good measure, pressed down, and shaken together, and running over, shall men give into your bosom.*

And then he read John 3:16. *For God so loved the world, that he gave his only begotten son, that whosoever believeth in him shall not perish, but have everlasting life.*

Two words stuck out to Bailey. *He. Gave.*

Gott—The Giver. Of everything good and holy and right. Of peace. Of joy. Of love. Of everlasting life.

THE END

Thanks for reading!
Word of mouth is one of the best forms of advertisement and a HUGE blessing to the author. If you enjoyed this book, **please** consider leaving a review, sharing on social media, and telling your reading friends.

THANK YOU!

DISCUSSION QUESTIONS

1. Bailey enjoys baking treats for her loved ones. Do you enjoy baking? If not, which hobbies are your favorite?

2. Bailey hadn't been expecting to run into Timothy. Have you ever run into someone from the past? A former love interest, perhaps?

3. Have you ever been involved in a similar shoebox project?

4. When Timothy discovers his *mammi* is depressed, he's unsure how to help her. Have you experienced depression after losing a loved one? How did you deal with it?

5. Holidays are often difficult when you've lost someone close because they're no longer there to celebrate with. Is there someone who may be lonely that you can reach

out to this holiday season?

6. When Timothy attempts to visit Mark at his work, he discovers something about Bailey's beau. Do you think he did the right thing in warning Bailey?

7. Have you ever been stranded in a snowstorm? How did you escape?

8. Have you ever had to forgive someone for past wrongs, even though their transgressions hurt you deeply?

9. Do you believe God has a perfect mate for most people? Why or why not?

10. What's different between the way the Amish in this book celebrate Christmas and the way you celebrate with your own family?

11. How do you keep Christ as the center of Christmas?

GET THE NEXT BOOK...

The Teacher (Amish Country Brides)

At the age of thirty-one, Martha Miller's chances of finding a life mate are basically nil in her Amish community. That is, until she reunites with her one-time friend, bachelor Jaden Beachy, at her niece's wedding. Maybe *Der Herr* hasn't forgotten about her status as a single woman after all. Although they agree to exchange letters after the wedding, he remains emotionally aloof and Martha is determined to find out why.

Jaden Beachy didn't expect to see Martha Miller ever again after her family moved from Pennsylvania to Indiana when the two of them were just scholars. Even at the tender age of eight, Jaden had been attracted to kind Martha. But Jaden carries a deep secret that he's never shared with anybody—a secret that could have Martha fleeing to the hills. When Jaden's older brother

Josiah informs him that their school is in need of a teacher, and invites him to come stay with him in Indiana, Jaden takes a leap of faith. Perhaps moving away can help him forget about his past failures. But living in the next district over from Martha's, along with their close family ties, will guarantee they'll run into each other.

Will Jaden dare share his secret with Martha? Or should he sever their relationship as soon as possible to save her from inevitable heartbreak?

NOW available for preorder!

A SPECIAL THANK YOU

I'd like to take this time to thank everyone that had any involvement in this book and its production, including my Mom and Dad, who have always been supportive of my writing, my longsuffering Family—especially my handsome, encouraging Hubby, my Amish and former-Amish friends who have helped immensely in my understanding of the Amish ways, my supportive Pastor and Church family, my Proofreaders, my Editor, my CIA Facebook author friends who have been a tremendous help, my wonderful Readers who buy, read, offer great input, and leave encouraging reviews and emails, my awesome Launch Team who, I'm confident, will 'Sprede the Word' about *The Drifter*! And last, but certainly not least, I'd like to thank my ***Precious LORD and SAVIOUR JESUS CHRIST***, for without Him, none of this would have been possible!

If you haven't joined my Facebook reader group, you may do so here:
www.facebook.com/groups/379193966104149/

An Unexpected Christmas Gift

Janie Mishler is content with her life as an *alt maedel* helping out at her father's Amish dry goods store, but she's always wondered "what if?" What if Elson hadn't passed on? What if she'd met someone else? What if she could raise a family of her own? But with each year that passes, Janie relinquishes her unfulfilled dreams. That is, until she receives an unexpected Christmas gift from someone who appears to be a stranger.

Rob Zehr put his Amish life behind him to forget about his painful past and follow his lifelong dream of becoming a pilot. Although he still communicates with his family, he has no desire to return to his old lifestyle. When he receives a mysterious note in the mail, he responds out of sheer intrigue. He never imagined that the note's writer could be the one to draw him back to his roots and open his heart to the possibility of love again.

Are their circumstances merely coincidence? Or could it be God's unseen hand working a Christmas miracle?

Made in United States
Troutdale, OR
08/20/2024

22184658R00141